BROKEN BOUNDARIES

A BROKEN REBEL BROTHERHOOD NOVEL

ANDI RHODES

Copyright © 2020 by Andi Rhodes

All rights reserved.

No part of this book may be reproduced in any form or by any electronic or mechanical means, including information storage and retrieval systems, without written permission from the author, except for the use of brief quotations in a book review.

Cover Artwork – © 2020 L.J. Anderson of Mayhem Cover Creations

For Courtney, my partner from day 1, my supporter, cheerleader, voice of reason, editor, sanity in the madness, and most importantly, my friend. Love ya, girl <3

ALSO BY ANDI RHODES

Broken Rebel Brotherhood

Broken Souls

Broken Innocence

Broken Boundaries

Broken Rebel Brotherhood: Complete Series Box set

Broken Rebel Brotherhood: Next Generation

Broken Hearts

Broken Wings

Broken Mind

Bastards and Badges

Stark Revenge

Slade's Fall

Jett's Guard

Soulless Kings MC

Fender

Joker

Piston

Greaser

Riker

Trainwreck

Squirrel

Gibson

Satan's Legacy MC

Snow's Angel

Toga's Demons

Magic's Torment

"The best relationships
are the ones you
never saw coming."

~Anonymous

PROLOGUE

AIDEN

*F*ucking weddings.

I hated them, but I was the best man so I had to be here. At least Micah and Griffin hadn't made me wear a monkey suit. That would have been pure torture. Griffin was currently arguing with his wife, Brie, and I was enjoying the show. Married a little over an hour and they were already fighting.

I sauntered over to the cake table to join them. "Aww, you guys having your first fight?" I slung my arms around their shoulders. "Tell papa Aiden all about it."

"Fuck off." Griffin elbowed me in the gut.

"Damn, man." I clutched my side, feigning hurt. Had Griffin put his full strength behind it, there would have been no pretending on my part. Brie was laughing at us, and I glared at her. "What's so funny?"

"You two. You're ridiculous." Her laughter continued for a few minutes, and I didn't have the heart to give her a hard time about it. She'd been through a lot recently, and it was great to see her happy.

Wanting to capture the moment, I pulled my phone out of

my pocket. "I want to get a picture of—" My eyes widened when I looked at the screen. "Fuck," I muttered.

"What is it?" Brie put her arm on mine and leaned over to look at the phone. "Who's Scarlett?"

"Uh, no one. Sorry, guys, but I've gotta go." I didn't bother looking up from the screen as I walked off and headed toward my bike.

When I reached Calypso, my Harley Davidson Street Bob, I straddled her and glanced at the text I'd received.

Scarlett: I hope u remember me. Need ur help. Meet me at Dusty's.

Did I remember her? Of course I fucking remembered her. I didn't bother taking the time to text her back before I pulled out of the driveway and pointed Calypso toward the little dive bar the brotherhood liked to frequent.

As I drove the country roads, I thought back to the day Scarlett had showed up asking for the help and protection of the Broken Rebel Brotherhood. She'd been twenty-three and drop-dead gorgeous. That had been two years ago, and at the time, she claimed to have a stalker. From the moment I answered the door to see her standing on the other side, I'd made mistake after mistake.

Rather than scheduling an appointment with her, like we always did with potential clients, I'd taken one look at her terrified demeanor and offered her a place to stay on BRB property, no questions asked. More precisely, I'd offered her a room in my own cabin.

Mistake number one.

At first, I'd stayed at the main house to give Scarlett privacy. Unfortunately, I found myself making up excuses to go see her. Sure, some of it had been legit. I'd needed to check on her, make sure she didn't need anything. I'd also had to get changes of clothes when I'd dirtied all I had at the main house.

Mistake number two.

Before I knew it, excuses were no longer necessary and I was back to staying at my own house, in my own bed… and she'd been in it with me.

Mistake number three.

I pulled into the parking lot at Dusty's and barely got the bike parked before hopping off and striding into the dimly lit bar.

"Yo, Aiden. Aren't you supposed to be at the wedding?" Dusty paused what he was doing and raised a hand in greeting.

"I was." I scanned the bar and noted there were fewer patrons than normal. *Probably all back at the reception.* My gaze landed back on Dusty's face. "Was there a woman in here? Blonde and about yea tall." I held my hand up in front of my chest to indicate Scarlett's height.

Dusty's eyes narrowed in thought. "Nope. Not that I recall." He swiveled around to yell back to the kitchen. "Hey, Kara! You see a blonde-haired chick in here at all tonight?"

Kara came through the swinging partition and gave me a cheeky grin. "Hey, Aiden."

She was beautiful, and at one time we'd had sex, but I had zero interest in a repeat performance. Not that she wasn't a nice woman, but there was only one female that I was interested in sharing a bed with long term and she'd taken off two years ago. "Can't say that I've seen any women here tonight. Everyone's at the wedding." Her hand was on her cocked hip as she spoke. "Who is she?"

Disappointment flooded my system. I rubbed the back of my neck and ignored Kara's question. Before sitting on a stool, I pulled my phone out of my pocket. "You sure? Name's Scarlett." I opened a photo I had saved and turned the phone for them to look at it. "This is an older picture, but I imagine she looks about the same." I hoped she looked the same.

Both shook their heads.

"Sorry, man," Dusty said. "Hey, you want a drink while you're here?" He bent to grab a glass from under the bar. "On the house."

"Yeah, sure." What I *really* wanted was to punch something. "Whatever is fine." I heaved a sigh and stared at Scarlett's photo. It had been taken one morning after breakfast. She was standing in front of the sink, rinsing dishes, and I'd made some smart-ass comment to get her to turn around. Her lips were slightly parted, and there were creases at the corners of her eyes because she'd laughed at whatever I'd said. My dick got hard, and I shifted on the stool.

Fuck this.

Me: Where r u? I'm at the bar.

I silently berated myself for texting her as I set the phone on the bar-top, screen down, and took a gulp of the ice-cold beer Dusty had sat in front of me. As the cool liquid settled in my gut, my phone pinged with an incoming text. I didn't immediately look at it. Instead, I ordered a shot of Fireball. As the whiskey burned a path down my throat, I felt a little more fortified and picked up my phone.

Scarlett: Sorry

Seriously? That's all she had to say? I raised two fingers in the air, indicating to Dusty that I wanted two more shots. When they were placed in front of me, I made short work of downing them both.

"You gonna need a ride home tonight, man?" Dusty's brows dipped in concern.

"Probably." I rarely drank to the point of oblivion, but I planned on it tonight. "Just don't call Micah or Griffin."

"Got it." He chuckled as he picked up the cordless phone to place a call. "Wouldn't want to interrupt the wedding night." He cackled, actually cackled, like an old gossipy woman. "Hey, Doc," he said into the phone. "Aiden's gonna need a ride tonight. Come get him in an hour or two?" I didn't hear the other side of the conversation, but I assumed Doc agreed.

And if he didn't? Fuck it. I'd be too drunk to give a damn where I slept, and the bar floor was as good a place as any.

1

AIDEN

Two years later...

Zzz... zzzz... zzzz.

My phone buzzed on my nightstand, and I rolled over, running into warm flesh.

"Mmm... make it stop." The woman's voice was whiny and for the life of me, I couldn't remember her name.

I crawled over her and winced when my cock dragged across her stomach and instantly hardened. My head was pounding, reminding me of the copious amounts of alcohol I'd consumed the night before.

Zzzz... zzzz... zzzz.

"Jesus, I'm coming," I muttered as I grabbed the device. There were several notifications of missed calls, and I scrubbed a hand over my face in the hopes that it would clear my bleary eyes.

"Not without me, honey." A hand came around my naked torso and fisted my dick.

My eyes dropped to take in the sight and rather than being turned on, all I felt was disgust. Unfortunately, my cock didn't get the memo. I gripped the small hand in mine and pulled it away from my body, glancing over my shoulder to give a placating smile as I did. "Not now."

"You're an asshole." The venom in the woman's words didn't stop me from standing to stalk to the bathroom. The pillow that hit the back of my head, however, did.

I took a deep breath before turning around and facing the bitch in my bed. "Get out." My voice was tight and if looks could kill, she'd have been a smoldering pile of ash.

"Are you fucking kidding me?" The woman crossed her arms over her plump breasts. I tried not to look, really I did, but my eyes dipped and narrowed when I noticed the hickeys covering her tits.

Jesus.

"No, I'm not kidding." I forced my gaze to return to her face, and my anger ratcheted up a notch at the pout I saw. I sighed and tried to level my emotions. "Look, it's been... fun. But I don't do mornings after." I mentally winced when I noticed that it was only four in the morning. Still morning though. "And I certainly don't put up with my own shit being thrown at me. So, I'll say it one more time." I paused, hoping she was getting the message. "Get. Out."

My phone chose that moment to start buzzing again, and when I glanced at the screen, I recognized the phone number. It was the hospital.

What the fuck?

"Hello," I said, after hitting the green button. I was dimly aware of my date, if you could even call her that, stomping around my room, trying to find her clothes.

"Hello. Is this Mr. Winters?" The voice sounded frazzled, and I instantly felt guilty for not answering my phone earlier.

"Yeah. I'm Aiden Winters." My eyes tracked the pissed off female's movements. *What was her name?*

I lost track of what the woman on the phone was saying as I tried to recall who the fuck I'd slept with. "Lisa." I snapped my fingers as her name finally came to me.

"Excuse me," the voice on the phone said at the same time Lisa's eyes snapped to mine.

"Nothing. Sorry," I mumbled. "What's this about Miss…?"

"Slater. Anna Slater. I'm a social worker at the hospital."

"Right. What can I do for you, Miss Slater?" As I spoke to the social worker, I watched as Lisa, now fully clothed, thank God, grabbed her purse off the floor and stormed out of the room. A few seconds later the front door slammed, and I sighed as the windows rattled.

"Well, Mr. Winters—"

"Aiden." Mr. Winters made me feel older than my thirty-five years.

"Aiden," Miss Slater repeated. "Do you know a Miss Scarlett Runyon?"

My whole body tensed at the name. "What's this about?"

"Please, answer the question Mr… Aiden." Miss Slater's voice was tinged with frustration.

"Yes, I know her." Images of Scarlett filtered into my brain. "At least, I did." I hadn't seen or spoken to her in four years. There was that one text, but other than that, radio silence. I'd spent a lot of that time trying to find her. I told myself—and the other members of the BRB—that it was because I wanted to protect her, but that had been a bald-faced lie. What time I hadn't spent trying to locate her, I'd spent trying to fuck her memory away.

"I'm sorry to have to tell you this, but Miss Runyon was admitted several hours ago and is currently in emergency surgery." Her words settled in my gut like a lead weight.

"Emergency surgery? What the hell happened?"

"I think it would be best if you came to the hospital to discuss the particulars. Are you able to come in?" The way she said that, it was like she was keeping something from me. Something important.

"Uh, yeah." My hand absently threaded through my hair. I mentally calculated how long it would take me to get there and then added twenty minutes to give me time to shower and wash away last night's debauchery. "I can be there in an hour."

"Thank you, Mr. Winters." I couldn't have corrected her even if I'd wanted to. So many scenarios played out in my mind, none of them good. "When you arrive, please let the front desk know you're here and they'll page me."

"Got it."

"See you soon, Mr. Winters." With that, she hung up.

I stuck my phone out in front of me and stared at the screen for a moment. After several seconds, I shook my head, as if to shake the answers loose to the million questions I had.

When the haze of confusion lifted, I grabbed clothes from my dresser and went to shower. I let myself linger under the spray a little longer than necessary, trying to get my swirling thoughts under control. It didn't work.

As I drove Calypso, my bike, to the hospital, all of my questions resurfaced.

Why did Scarlett need emergency surgery?

Why was she back in Indiana?

Where had she been the last four years?

And more importantly…

Why the fuck was the hospital calling me?

2

AIDEN

"Mr. Winters, Aiden, please, have a seat." Miss Slater was younger than I'd pictured based on our short conversation. "Can I get you anything to drink? Coffee? Water?"

"No, thanks. I'd really like to know why I'm here." I sat in the leather chair across the desk from her, balancing a boot on my knee. "I don't understand why I was called for Scarlett."

"I'll answer all of your questions, but first, I've got a few of my own." Her statement caused my unease to grow in its intensity.

"Ask away, although I'm not clear on what information I could possibly provide."

"I believe you'll understand soon enough." Miss Slater picked up a folder on her desk and leafed through the papers it contained. "Ah, here it is. Is this Scarlett Runyon?" She slid a black and white copy of a driver's license toward me.

I picked up the paper and glanced at it quickly. "It is. But you already knew that. It's a driver's license. It has her name on it." Anger began to replace my unease.

"We have to be sure."

"I see." But of course, I didn't. How bad were Scarlett's injuries that they couldn't be sure it was her they'd admitted? "What exactly are her injuries?"

"I'm afraid they're considerable. Extensive bruising, indicating she was beaten severely before arriving at the hospital." She glanced down at another paper and read from it. The list was long and made my head spin. "Oh, and a contusion on the brain. The contusion on the brain has caused significant swelling, which is the doctor's primary concern, at the moment."

"Jesus." Every scenario I'd imagined had not prepared me for the horror of that list.

The crack of my knuckles echoed in the office as Miss Slater finished talking. I hadn't realized I'd been popping them, and I clenched my fists to stop myself.

"The surgeon drilled a small hole into Ms. Runyon's skull to relieve some of the pressure. Once that was complete, they started addressing her other injuries. At this time, it's unclear whether or not she'll wake up." Miss Slater looked at me with sympathy. "The doctors are hopeful though, as she's breathing on her own."

"But they can't be sure?" *Please, God, let Scarlett wake up.*

"At this time, no." She shook her head and gave a sad smile. "I'm sorry."

As fast as the social worker answered my questions, another one surfaced. "How did she get here? As far as I know, she doesn't live in Indiana." My eyes searched hers as I spoke.

"We can't say for certain how she got here, but she was found in the ER parking lot."

The chair rocked as I surged to my feet. "What the fuck do you mean you 'found' her in the parking lot?" My palms slammed down on her desk, and she reared back at the sound.

"Mr. Winters, please, sit down." She'd been scared for a second, but quickly recovered. As she pointed to the chair behind me, her tone was downright *chilly,* and I instantly regretted my outburst. I straightened and crossed my arms over my chest, but I didn't sit. She seemed to recognize that was the most cooperation she was going to get from me because she didn't push the issue. "A nurse arrived for her shift around midnight and came across Miss Runyon as she was walking through the parking lot. And she wasn't alone."

"Why was she in the middle of—" My mouth slammed shut as her words registered. "Wait. Did you say she wasn't alone?"

Her lips parted to answer at the same time a knock sounded on the door. My eyes narrowed at the intrusion, but she ignored my obvious annoyance. "Come in," she called.

I turned around in time to watch a nurse enter. Gripping her hand was a little girl with blonde pigtails and clothes that had seen better days. The child was rubbing her eye with a tiny fist, and when she dropped her hand to her side, she peered up at me. She must have sensed the anger bubbling just under the surface because she shuffled her feet closer to the nurse, curled into her side and ducked her head.

"Aiden, this is Tillie." The social worker spoke from behind me, and as she did, the nurse mouthed 'sorry' to her.

It's Miss Slater's daughter. That had to be it. Why else would she have interrupted? With that thought in mind, I stepped toward the child and hunkered down, hoping that would make me less intimidating. I was pissed, but I wasn't going to take it out on her, and I certainly didn't want to scare her.

"Hi Tillie." I forced the tension from my body and smiled at her. "I'm Aiden."

Tillie's head came around the nurse's body. Her eyes widened and she gave me a small smile. "You're the man fwom the picture."

"Picture? What picture?" My brow dipped with confusion. How had Tillie seen a picture of me?

"The picture mommy shows me." Tillie ducked back behind the nurse before I could question her further.

I stood up to my full height and whirled on Miss Slater. "What is she talking about? How does she recognize me?"

"Aiden, please, calm down," she said, nodding toward the little girl I'd no doubt scared. "When I said Miss Runyon gave us your name, I failed to mention that she gave us your name when she was asked if there was anyone we could call to care for Tillie."

A growl erupted from me. "Why would she do that?"

"I can answer that." My head swiveled to see Jackson crossing the threshold to the room, holding a file. He pinned me with his stare, gaining my full attention. "Scarlett gave them your name because," Jackson took a deep breath and with only two more words, changed my life forever. "Tillie's yours."

After Jackson had dropped his bombshell, I'd been shocked. I couldn't force my head to rise. Everyone's feet swam in my confusion hazed vision. And so much rage flowed through my system because Jackson hadn't called me immediately.

"Mr. Winters… Aiden, are you okay?" Miss Slater's hand touched my arm as I shook my head. "Stella, can you please get Aiden some water?" I assumed she was talking to the nurse because her shoes disappeared from my line of sight. Tillie's shoes remained where they were. Her very small, tattered, pink shoes.

"I want mommy." My head snapped up at the words, and the tears in Tillie's eyes leveled me. Her bottom lip poked out and quivered. I'd been around Micah's twins enough to recognize what was about to happen. Any second, the tears would fall and it would be next to impossible to stop the crying. Tillie surprised me, though. The sheen in her eyes disappeared and rather than give in to her fear, she crossed her arms over her chest and stomped her foot. "I want my mommy."

Well, shit. I glanced at Jackson, who only shrugged.

"I know, peanut," I said as I knelt in front of her. Where the nickname came from, I had no idea. It just sort of slipped out. "But your mommy is..." I glanced over my shoulder at Miss Slater, silently begging her to fill in the blanks for me. I had no idea what to tell a child in this situation.

"Mommy has an owie." Tillie's tiny voice held an innocence that I hoped wouldn't be shattered by this whole situation.

Stella came back in, carrying a bottle of water, and handed it to me.

"Thanks," I muttered, grateful for the interruption. I unscrewed the cap and took a long drink, letting the cool liquid ease the fire in me.

"Tillie, why don't you go with Stella? I'm sure she can find some coloring books and crayons for you." Miss Slater gave a pointed look to Stella, who proceeded to usher Tillie out of the office. "Aiden?" I was still kneeling, staring at the closed door. My head fell to my chest before I heaved myself up and turned to face her.

Now that Tillie was gone, my outrage spiked and I allowed my doubt to take over. "Miss Slater, I don't know why Scarlett thought I should be called but," my gaze swung to Jackson, "I'm not a father. Tillie isn't my daughter." I shook my head as I spoke

"Aiden, man, I hate to be the one to break it to you, but you are her father." Jackson shuffled through the folder he was holding before thrusting a single piece of paper at me.

I stared at his outstretched hand, afraid to reach out and grab the document. Jackson shook it in front of me, and I snatched it from him. I skimmed over the words, freezing on one line:

Father: Aiden Winters

"I don't understand." This had to be a joke. The Brotherhood was playing a prank. Never mind that pranks weren't their thing. It was the *only* thing that made sense.

"When Miss Runyon was found, we immediately called law enforcement in becau—"

"I know how the damn law works." Miss Slater's eyes narrowed at me. "I don't understand why she kept this from me." My voice boomed in the small office as I looked back and forth between Anna and Jackson.

"After I got the call from Miss Runyon, I went back to the station to do some digging. I was able to pull Tillie's birth certificate to verify everything. I knew you wouldn't just take anyone's word for it that you're her father." Jackson looked at me with sympathy, and in that moment, I hated him.

"Aiden, if this is too much for you, I can call social—"

"No," I snapped.

"Services and," she continued as if I hadn't just cut her off. "they can find a foster home while—"

"I said 'no'." My heartbeat thundered so loud I was sure they heard it as clearly as I felt it. "I'm her father and she'll stay with me." I had no idea what I was doing, but I'd be damned if a child of mine went into foster care. I'd grown up in foster homes and wouldn't wish it on my worst enemy.

"Aiden, you need to take time to think about this. A child

is a big responsibility." Jackson took several deep breaths before continuing. "Why don't you take a few days to think about it? Tillie will be placed in a temporary home during that time."

"Look, my name is on this birth certificate." I gripped the document in my hand tighter. "She's coming home with me. That *is* why you called me, right?"

"Well, yes, but—"

"But nothing."

"Aiden, do you even have a car seat to take her home in?" Leave it to Jackson to point out a flaw in my plan. One of many.

Fuck!

Of course I didn't have a damn car seat and he knew it. I'd driven here on Calypso. Maybe they were right. Maybe I had no idea what I was doing. But I knew who could help me. I yanked my phone out of my pocket and hit the speed dial I needed.

"Micah," I barked into the phone when he answered. "I need you at the hospital. Now. And bring a damn car seat with you."

3

AIDEN

"You wanna tell me what this is all about?" Micah entered the hospital, his shoulders slumped and eyes heavy with exhaustion. I had a moment of regret for pulling him out of bed, but when my eyes landed on the pink car seat in his hand, regret took a backseat to everything else.

"I don't even know where to start." I lowered my head and shuffled my feet.

After I'd gotten off the phone with him, shame had washed over me. Not only had I broken my own moral code — never sleep with a client — but I'd also broken the unspoken code of the BRB. Sleeping with Scarlett had been the epitome of stupid. I couldn't bring myself to go so far as to say I wished it hadn't happened, but it was close.

"Try the beginning. That seems like the logical place." He stood there staring at me, patiently waiting me out.

"Do you remember Scarlett?" If he wanted the beginning, I'd take him to the beginning.

"Pretty little thing with a stalker, right?" His forehead creased, as if trying to conjure up an image of her.

I had no such problem. The image of her five foot two frame was emblazoned on my brain. She had legs that were built to be wrapped around a man's hips, tits made for sucking and a mouth designed to devour. Her blonde hair and baby blue eyes were icing on the cake.

"Right." I gripped his arm and pulled him toward the seats in the waiting room, forcing the image away with a shake of my head as I walked. I picked two chairs in an empty corner. This was no one else's damn business and this was the closest thing to privacy we were going to get. After we sat, I leaned my head back against the wall and looked at the ceiling. I couldn't look him in the eye for this next part. "I slept with her."

"Okay. I had to bring a car seat with me, so I'm guessing the story doesn't end there." I still hadn't looked at him, but I could feel his stare burning into my skin.

"Ding ding ding, give the man a prize." I've been told I always used humor as a defense mechanism, and I used it now like a damn shield.

When Micah didn't say anything, I forced my gaze to meet his and was shocked at the smile on his face. My eyes widened as I shook my head, as if that would change the image before me. "What's so funny?"

"You, brother." His hand rested on my shoulder as he spoke. "If you could see your face right now… priceless." Laughter tinged his voice, but he didn't let it out. "Let me guess, you thought I'd come here and lay into you about sleeping with a client?"

"Well, yeah." I was so confused. "I crossed so many boundaries and now I have a daughter." The reality of that statement hit me like a sucker punch. Saying it out loud to someone made it real.

"First things first. Maybe four years ago I'd have jumped your shit but, Sadie, man." He looked out across the room, but his eyes weren't focused on anything directly in front of him. It was like he mentally transported himself to a different time and place. "I'd be nothing without her, and our relationship wasn't exactly… conventional." His eyes focused back in on me. "Second, you've got a daughter. That's something incredible and you should never be sorry about that."

"Tillie. Her name's Tillie." I cracked the first real smile since I'd arrived at the hospital. God, that felt like a lifetime ago. "Damn, Micah, she's the cutest thing I've ever seen. Curly blonde hair in pigtails. The bluest eyes you've ever seen and a cherubic face. She's like a little pixie, and she's got spunk."

Micah threw his head back and laughed. A deep belly laugh that caught me off guard.

"What?" I narrowed my eyes at him.

"You're so fucked, dude. If she's anything like my Izzy, you're gonna have your hands full." His laughter subsided and he got serious. "When can I meet her?"

"Soon, but first, I need to fill you in on Scarlett." I listed her injuries, ticking them off with my fingers as I did. "I haven't seen her yet. She was still in surgery when I got here but shit, man, it's gotta be bad. And Tillie saw that. Who does that? Drops off an unconscious woman in a parking lot with a fucking kid!" Several heads turned our way at my raised voice.

"Brother, some people are just evil. There's no other explanation." He stood and picked up the car seat. "Let's go see Scarlett first, and then you can introduce me to Tillie."

"Shit. I haven't even been introduced to her. Not really." I couldn't believe I hadn't thought of that before now. "What if she hates me? What if she already has a 'daddy'?" The air in the hospital was suddenly too thick to enter my lungs.

"Aiden, breathe." Micah put his hand on my shoulder again. "She's gonna love you. She might be scared or nervous at first, but she'll come around. Don't get me wrong, you've definitely got a rough road ahead of you, but that's what the rest of us are here for. We've got your back."

"Thanks, man." I shoved my fingers through my hair. I'd done that a lot, and it probably showed. "Let me see if someone can tell us her room number." I walked to the nurse's station and asked for the information. When I had it, Micah and I took the elevator to the fifth floor, where we met Anna.

"Hi. I'm Anna Slater, the social worker." She stuck her hand out for Micah to shake. When he did so, she continued. "And you are...?"

"Micah, ma'am. I'm Aiden's brother."

"I wasn't aware Aiden had any family." Anna looked from Micah to me, questions dancing in her eyes.

"He does." Micah's tone was challenging. He might not be family by blood, but he was family in every way that mattered.

"Well, then, I'm sure he's got a great support system in place to help with Tillie."

"Absolutely." I glared at Micah as I interrupted, hoping he'd catch on to shut the hell up. Micah's frustration was palpable, and I was afraid that if this conversation went on much longer, he'd do or say something regretful.

"Ma'am, I'm the father of two children. Four-year-old twins, Isabelle and Isaiah." Micah hadn't caught on. "Then there's my wife, Sadie, and our friends..."

Anna's eyes appeared to glaze over as Micah listed the names of BRB members. He was clearly pissed that someone would question a brother's ability to raise a child, and while I appreciated the sentiment, he was being ridiculous.

"Anna, I'd really like to see Scarlett, if you don't mind." Time to take back control of this situation.

"Of course," she responded. "She was just settled into her room. Follow me, please."

We followed her down the sterile corridor until she stopped in front of a closed door. Room five seventeen. I committed the number to memory, certain I'd be spending a lot of time here.

"Aiden, she still hasn't woken up, but she continues to breathe on her own, so the doctors remain hopeful for a full recovery." With that, she opened the door and stepped aside for Micah and me to enter. "I'll leave you alone for a bit. Come to my office when you're done." With that, she turned and walked away.

Micah walked through the doorway before I did. My feet were glued to the floor. The light in the room was dim, but I was able to make out the still form lying in the bed and I was afraid to see her clearly. I knew it would be bad, and that wasn't how I wanted to picture Scarlett.

"You coming?" Micah's voice broke through my thoughts, and my eyes snapped to his.

My feet finally carried me into the room, stopping short when Scarlett came fully into view. "Jesus Christ," I whispered. Rage simmered below the surface, mixing in with shock at the reality of her condition.

"Any idea who did this?" Micah's tone held the same rage I felt. No doubt seeing Scarlett brought back memories of when he'd found his wife beaten and bloody.

I wasn't capable of speech, so I shook my head. I took a few steps, closing the distance between myself and the woman who'd haunted my existence for the last four years. Her face was barely recognizable, it was so bruised and swollen. I closed my eyes and conjured up an image of her the last time I'd seen her. Beautiful, smiling, *satisfied.*

With that image in mind, I opened my eyes and let my gaze

glide over her body. There wasn't an inch of unharmed flesh visible. She was partially covered by a white sheet, and I imagined the pallor of her skin would blend in with it if it wasn't colored in blue and purple hues. The IV she was hooked up to pushed a steady stream of medication into her system, and the monitors beeped in a reassuring tone. She was alive.

As I stood there, memorizing every injury, every bruise, scratch, scrape, I thought of Tillie. "Fuck, Tillie saw this." I shook my head, as if doing so would make it less true.

"Damn," Micah muttered. "Kids are resilient, though. Maybe she won't remember." He almost sounded as if he were asking a question, but I knew it was more of a prayer. Because that's what it would take for Tillie not to remember. A thousand prayers.

I said my first one.

Please, God, don't let this be burned into Tillie's memory.

I'd do anything it took to make her forget. No child should have to see their mother like this. Another thought hit me like a freight train.

It must have hit Micah at the same time because he was the one to voice the question. "Did Tillie see this actually happen? Or just the aftermath?"

"Shit, I don't know." I glanced at Micah in time to see his jaw harden. "I need answers. Yesterday." The words tore out of me.

"We'll get them," Micah assured me. He was good at that. Making a statement in such a way that forced you to believe him, no matter how unsure you really were.

I pulled a chair up to the bed and sat, leaning over the edge as I did. I gently held Scarlett's much smaller hand in mine. "You gotta wake up, sugar. Our daughter is going to need you." I had no idea if she could hear me, but I had to try. "She's beautiful, Scarlett." My eyes glazed over with unshed tears. I swiped at them, embarrassed because I wasn't normally an emotional man.

The longer I sat there, the less I felt like crying and the angrier I became. At the situation, at the depravity of it, at *her*. "How could you do this? Why didn't you tell me about Tillie?"

"Aiden, you'll get a chance to ask all those questions, but not now." Micah's voice quieted some of the anger in my head. "Don't say anything now that you might regret later. You feel me?"

I swallowed past the emotions and nodded. "I feel you." He was right. He didn't want me to say anything I would regret if she didn't wake up. If she died. I returned my focus to Scarlett. "Sugar, you got this. Be the fighter I know you to be. Come back to Tillie."

I blew out a breath before whispering my last plea. "Come back to me."

4

SCARLETT

Why did that voice sound so familiar?

I heard the pleas for me to wake up, and in an effort to do just that, I struggled against the weight on my lids. Something flowed through my system, making me feel groggy, and I had no idea what it was. Very slowly, light filtered into my line of vision, as I was able to crack my eyes open. I tried to open them further, but it was impossible. *Why?*

"Uh, bro, I think she's awake." A voice I vaguely recognized broke into the silence, and I turned my head toward it, frustrated at the pain that followed.

"Hey, sugar. Welcome back." Recognition hit immediately as the familiar pet name registered.

A large hand curled around my much smaller one, and I attempted to yank it back but found the movement impossible. I tilted my head down to see what held me immobile and was confused to see the cast on my arm. Hundreds of questions flooded my brain, but I wasn't able to put voice to a single one. I glanced back up at Aiden and tried to convey my confusion to him. He had always been able to read me better than anyone, and I was banking on his ability to still do so.

"What's wrong, sugar?" His voice was laced with concern, and the anger I'd heard before fully coming into consciousness was gone.

"H… wha…" I slowly shook my head in frustration.

"Do you know where you are?" The other man in the room stepped behind Aiden, into my line of view.

I shook my head and fought the dizziness that washed over me.

"You're in the hospital. Do you have any idea how you got here?"

Again, I shook my head. I dropped my gaze to the bed, trying to piece together what had happened and how I'd ended up in the hospital with a cast on my arm. The last thing I remembered was Justin standing at our front door when Tillie and I had gotten home after a long day of work and daycare. He'd found us, *again*. We'd argued about Tillie—

My head snapped up to look at Aiden at the thought of my daughter. An incessant beeping filled the room, and Aiden stood up, fear entering his expression.

"Sugar, you need to calm down." He leaned over me and brushed kisses across my forehead. "Please, calm down."

I frantically shook my head and forced words out of my mouth. "Till… where's…"

"Tillie's fine. She's with the social worker." Aiden smoothed my hair back, and I winced when he touched a particularly tender spot. His face quickly went from calm and reassuring to tight and controlled. "How could you keep her from me?"

"Aiden," the other man snapped. "Not the time."

"Right. Fine." Aiden blew out a breath before taking another deeper one. "We'll talk about it later. For now, just know that's she's safe."

I started to sit up, but black spots danced around my head, so I let myself fall back against the pillows. "I need—"

"I'll bring her to you in a bit." Aiden's sharp words cut me off. I understood his anger, but I did *not* need it then.

I nodded and allowed the tension to leave my body. "Thanks."

"No problem."

Aiden took a step away from the bed, breaking the contact with me, and I instantly missed his heat. His comfort. I had loved him once, but I'd made a choice to leave and regardless of my current situation, I stood by that choice. Why then, did I want to feel his body next to mine and soak up anything he had to offer?

"I'm going to go get the doctor. Let them know you're awake." Aiden turned on his heel and walked out the door.

I turned to look at the other man in the room and watched as his gaze followed Aiden out before he turned back to me and sighed.

"I'm Micah." He took a step toward the bed. "You don't remember me, do you?"

I thought for a minute before shaking my head.

"I'm the president of the BRB. We met when you stayed at Aiden's a few years ago."

My brain was still a little fuzzy, and I hated that I couldn't recall any memory of the man.

"It's okay. It'll all come back to you once you've recovered."

"Will it?" I prayed it would because I did not want amnesia on top of whatever the fuck else had happened. In that moment though, I was scared that my memory wouldn't all come back.

"Sure it will. You have to believe that." He smiled, and just like that, a memory surfaced. Of him introducing himself to me years ago.

"I remember," I croaked.

Micah chuckled. "See, told ya."

"Told her what?" Aiden stepped up beside Micah, and a doctor walked around to the other side of the bed.

"That she'd remember me."

Aiden's eyes narrowed for a split second before he plastered a smile on his face.

"We're going to let the doctor check you out and go talk to the social worker." He had grabbed my hand, and I squeezed as hard as I could to let him know I didn't want him to leave. "We'll be back. And we'll bring Tillie." He squeezed my hand in reassurance, and when my grip loosened, he dropped my hand to the bed and he and Micah were gone.

5

AIDEN

"Aiden, are you ready for me to get Tillie?" Miss Slater, Anna, looked at me expectantly. Micah and I had been back in her office for fifteen minutes, going over the details, again, of how Scarlett was found and her present condition and prognosis. Scarlett had only woken up while Micah and I had been with her, and it would take time to figure out what all happened.

"In a minute. I have one question that hasn't been addressed yet." Micah spoke to Anna, but glanced at me.

"And what's that?" she asked.

"Have the cops been called?" Anna's eyes widened as if the question was absurd. It probably was… in her world. In ours, not so much.

"Of cour "

"Shit!" I interrupted her. "I forgot to tell you Jackson was here earlier." I gave Micah an apologetic look before my gaze returned to Anna.

Her indignation turned to frustration as she glared at me before returning her attention to Micah. "Why would you even think otherwise?"

"In our line of work, you never know. Rarely are the cops called unless it's by one of us." Micah smiled in what I imagined was his way of placating the social worker.

"I see. Well, I'm not real clear on what it is you do, although the sheriff tried to explain, but…" Neither Micah nor I provided an answer to the unspoken question.

"Can you please get my daughter?" As nervous as I was about being a father, I didn't want to spend longer than necessary in this office, dealing with Anna's questions.

Rather than answer, Anna picked up the phone on her desk and punched in a few numbers. "Stella, would you please bring Tillie to my office?" She nodded and as she listened to Stella talk, her brow furrowed, and she peered at Micah. "Yes, of course. Bring her with you." More nodding. "That would be great. Thank you, Stella." She hung up the phone before resting her elbows on the desk and folding her hands.

"Something wrong?" Micah asked.

Anna didn't respond, but rather her eyes went from Micah to me.

"What?" My patience was slipping.

She took a deep breath and blew it out, then shook her head. "Nothing."

"Look, Miss Slater, if you've got something to say, spit it out." Micah's voice was commanding, and Anna's jaw dropped.

She pulled herself together, and her professionalism took control. "I'm concerned about Tillie. She's obviously witnessed violence and I do not want to put her in a situation where she may be surrounded by it."

Both Micah and I came out of our chairs, which only served to give her more reason to be concerned. I forced myself to calm down before I dared to speak, but Micah beat me to it.

"Miss Slater, don't for one second let our *rough* demeanor fool you." For someone who didn't know Micah well, he appeared calm, cool and collected. All *I* saw was the tension and the seething rage he was trying desperately to hide. "We may not look like it, but you won't find a more dedicated group of people, and every last one of us will protect Tillie... with our lives, if necessary. She will be loved more than you could possibly fathom. Hell, Aiden probably loves her already, and he's only seen her for what? Two minutes?"

Fuck.

Was he right? Did I already love her?

Yes.

All it had taken was one look at her and a quick glance at the birth certificate, and Tillie had me. Hook, line, and sinker. She was a part of me, and there wasn't anything on this Earth that could keep me from her. Four years had already been stolen from me, but no more.

A soft knock sounded on the door, causing my heart rate to skyrocket. Anna glanced toward the door and then back to us. Indecision skittered across her features before she finally settled on a look of resignation. She'd lost this battle. I just prayed she didn't later decide to start a war.

"Come in," she called.

I turned toward the door and was dimly aware of Micah mimicking my actions. The same nurse from earlier, Stella, walked through the door. Behind her, Sadie came in, with Tillie tightly clinging to her arm.

Tillie's eyes peered up at me and then to Micah. When her gaze landed on him, she shrank back behind Sadie.

"Sadie, what—"

"I texted her." My head swiveled toward Micah and he shrugged. "Thought she could help."

"But..." Confusion swirled in my brain, but one look at Tillie and it began to melt away. She appeared relaxed with

Sadie at her side. If Sadie could help Tillie, then who was I to argue about the hows and whys?

Decision made to accept Sadie's presence as a good thing, I focused on Tillie. "Hey, peanut," I spoke softly as I walked toward her, crouching down when I reached her. "Remember me?"

She glanced back up at Micah, and after several seconds, she looked at me and nodded. "I member. I seen you lots of times."

I chuckled at the way she spoke. "Right. The *picture*." I reached out and when she flinched, I froze. *Oh, hell no.* Rage seeped through my pores, but I didn't dare let Tillie see it. She was scared enough.

Sadie knelt down and wrapped her arm around Tillie's shoulder before leaning in and whispering something in the child's ear. Tillie giggled and I glanced at Micah, taking in his shaking head and wide smile. Thank God for good friends who knew exactly what to do no matter what the situation. I wouldn't have even thought to get Sadie here, but Micah had.

"Tillie, can I talk to you for a minute?" Anna crouched next to me. When Tillie nodded, Anna held out her hand and Tillie grabbed it.

I watched as they walked to a couch, Tillie glancing over her shoulder at me the entire time. It was almost as if she feared letting me out of her sight. Maybe the photo she'd seen was a good thing. At least *I* was familiar to *her,* even if her existence was a shock to me. When Tillie struggled to get up on the couch, I had to force myself to hold back. The couch was a little tall for her, and I desperately wanted to help her, ease *any* difficulty she faced.

As Anna spent time talking to Tillie about nothing important, I glanced at Sadie. Her eyes were trained on me and they were soft. I mouthed 'thank you' to her, and she simply smiled before walking to Micah and leaning into his side. The two were so much in love that, despite where we were, I had to turn away because I felt as if I were intruding on an intimate moment.

My attention returned to Anna and my daughter. Even though I'd missed a lot of the conversation, Anna's tone had my shoulders stiffening.

"Well," Anna smiled at Tillie and I knew, I just *knew*, what was coming. "Aiden is your father. Do you know what that means?"

Tillie nodded. I hadn't missed the wide eyes that had appeared at the word 'father'. Tension seeped from my shoulders through the rest of my body as jealousy coursed through me. I hated that there might be a man out there who she already thought was her dad, and I was fucking pissed. I had no idea what Tillie's life had been like up until that point. Did she already have a dad? Would me being in her life just confuse her? I shook my head to rid myself of the thoughts. I'd get answers soon.

"Because he's your father, he's going to be taking care of you while mommy is resting." That was an oversimplification if I ever heard one.

Her eyes went wide, and she shook her head. So many more questions rose to the surface, but I resisted the urge to rattle them off. I followed her gaze as she looked to Sadie.

Sadie walked toward the couch and sat on Tillie's other side. "Tillie, remember what we talked about before we came in?"

Tillie glanced up at Sadie, and she appeared to think about the question before bobbing her head up and down. I had no idea what they had talked about, but whatever it was seemed to be calming for Tillie.

"And I promised, didn't I?" Sadie's voice was patient, friendly, but also… motherly.

Again, Tillie nodded.

"Ah, sweetness? What exactly did you promise?" Micah's voice startled Tillie, but I had been thinking the same question and was glad he'd asked it.

"Tillie," Sadie peered into my daughter's eyes as she spoke, "why don't you tell them what I promised?" When Tillie said nothing, Sadie nudged her with her shoulder. "Go ahead, you can tell them anything."

"She says she stay wif me." Tillie's voice was barely above a whisper.

Sadie glanced at me and then to Micah, practically daring us to contradict her. Micah's eyes narrowed slightly, but he knew better than to argue. And quite frankly, so did I. "That's right. Anytime you need me or you feel scared, I'll be there."

"Peanut, would it make you feel better if Sadie was with you?" I'd been standing back, content to let Sadie handle this conversation, but I couldn't do that anymore. I went to the couch and crouched in front of Tillie, ignoring the way her tiny body scooted closer to Sadie. Sure, she'd seen a picture of me, but I was still a stranger and after what happened to Scarlett, I didn't blame her for being scared.

Tillie buried her face in Sadie's side, but she nodded.

I had no clue as to the logistics of making that work, but if that's what it took to make Tillie comfortable with me, then I'd make it happen. "Okay."

"Good. Now, Tillie, remember who he is?" Sadie asked as she pointed to Micah.

Tillie peered at Micah and then me before settling her gaze back on Sadie and shaking her head.

"He's my husband. And completely safe." Sadie hugged Tillie tight in an effort to reassure her. "We have a little girl that's your age. And a little boy." She looked to Micah and smiled. "His name's Micah. Can he come here and say 'hi'?"

Micah waited for her to give the 'okay' and when she nodded, he came and crouched next to me. "Hey, munchkin."

He stuck his hand out for her to shake. She stared at it for a moment, never leaving the comfort of Sadie's side, before reaching out and allowing her tiny hand to be swallowed up by his much larger one. "It's nice to meet you."

"You're big," she said. The room erupted in laughter, and just like that, some of the tension eased.

"I guess I am," he said when the laughter subsided. "But I'm not so scary, am I?" He made faces at her, trying to put her at ease. It worked. She giggled and shook her head.

"Tillie, would it be okay if you stayed with me for a while?" It wasn't as if she really had a choice in the matter, but I didn't want her to know that.

"What about mommy?" Leave it to a child to ask an impossible question.

"Well—"

"Mommy's going to stay here so she can get some rest," Micah interrupted. I mouthed 'thank you' to him because really, he'd saved me. I'd had no clue how to answer that question.

"I wanna see mommy." Tillie's bottom lip poked out.

I looked at Anna and gauged her reaction. She didn't appear to think it was a bad idea, so I went with my gut instinct.

"We can go see your mommy before we leave." She deserved to see Scarlett. I couldn't deny her that opportunity. I just prayed that I could help her work through whatever emotion seeing her might cause.

Her face scrunched up as she considered my words. "Can I have toys?"

"Of course. We'll get you some today." I'd do anything she asked.

I'm so fucked.

"'Kay." She hopped off the couch and marched toward the door, tugging Sadie along with her, momentarily forgetting the fear. When she reached the closed barrier, she turned to face me. "C'mon."

"Go ahead. I'll make sure everything is in order before you're all ready to leave." Anna stood from the couch and walked to her desk. "Just stop back by before you go."

I made my way to Tillie and when she cautiously placed her free hand in mine, my eyes snapped to Micah. Micah had a shit-eating grin on his face. *Fucker.*

6

SCARLETT

It was all I could do to keep my eyes open, but Aiden had said he would bring Tillie to see me, and I wanted to be awake when she came in. My lids fluttered closed and just as I was about to lose the battle—

"Mommy!" My eyes snapped open, and I turned my head toward the one and only voice that gave me reason to keep fighting. I forced the pain to the back of my mind and focused on the little sunshine that came barreling into my room.

"Hey, baby." I winced at the croak in my voice but had to accept the fact that I couldn't help it.

Tillie ran to my bedside and reached her tiny hands over the edge to grab me. When she shook my arm, I didn't have it in my heart to tell her to stop or that she was hurting me, so I forced a smile and hoped it reached my eyes.

"Hey, peanut." Resentment flooded my system as Aiden's voice broke the connection between Tillie and me. My gaze slid to Aiden as he walked toward us and sat in the chair. "Why don't you sit on my lap and you can talk to mommy?"

Aiden patted his leg. Tillie's eyes darted between him and me, silently asking for my permission.

Oh, how I wanted to deny her, to keep her to myself and not share. But I couldn't. He was her father, and although I had my reasons for keeping her from him, my time had run out. She needed someone to look after her while I was in the hospital, and I was afraid I would need him just as much after I was released.

"It's okay, baby. Go ahead." Permission granted, Tillie twisted away from me and scrambled up to sit on Aiden's lap.

The sight of them, of father and daughter together, shifted something in me. It felt like the blade that I'd shoved into my heart when I'd left Aiden was slowly being pulled out, easing my heartache slightly. I mentally shoved it back in, not trusting the foreign feeling.

My hands fisted the sheet, and I turned away before either of them could see the lone tear that slipped down my cheek.

"Hi, mommy." I took as deep a breath as my constricting chest would allow before turning back to face her. "I haf to stay wif him so you can west." She hitched her thumb over her shoulder indicating Aiden. "But don't worry. Sadie's gonna be wif me."

Sadie? Jealousy snaked through my system and manifested itself into a scowl.

"Who's Sadie?" My eyes snapped to Aiden, and that's when Micah and a woman came into my line of vision behind him. A very beautiful woman.

Micah chuckled. "Scarlett, Sadie's my wife." He slung his arm around the woman at his side, Sadie I presumed, and pulled her close. She blushed at his words, but not from embarrassment or nerves. No, it was from something I hadn't felt in a long time. Not since Aiden. It was love. Real love.

"Oh." My head throbbed and the emotional whiplash didn't help. "Well…" I had no idea what to say.

"Hi Scarlett." The woman under Micah's arm stepped away from him and toward me. "I'm Sadie. I… lived with the BRB when you were there before."

Her voice was soft, but I hadn't missed the hesitation. There was a story there, I was sure of it, but those details would have to wait for another time.

"Oh, um, hi. It's nice to meet you."

"You're probably wondering why I'm here." She spoke with a little more authority this time. More confidence.

"Maybe a little. I mean, I know why Aiden's here, but—" I snapped my mouth shut. Did I really know why Aiden was there? *Not really.* I didn't even know how *I* had gotten there. I flicked my eyes to Aiden's and held his stare. After several seconds, I found my voice again. "Why are you here?"

He shifted in the chair, looking as uncomfortable as I felt. A storm cloud swirled around him, despite the sunlight he held in his arms, and it scared me. I'd been through countless storms the last few years and didn't have it in me to figure out how to dance through another one.

"I think a better question is, why haven't I been here until now?" He finally responded.

Ouch.

"That's enough." Micah's tone was forceful. "This isn't the time or the place. We've been through this, Aiden."

"Mommy?" The insecurity in my daughter's voice told me that Micah was right. This wasn't the time or place to have this discussion.

"Yes, baby?"

"I wanna stay wif you." Her bottom lip trembled, and I

ached to reach out to her and comfort her. But I couldn't. Not in my condition.

"I know baby, but your... Aiden's going to take really good care of you." I couldn't bring myself to call him what he was. Her father. I didn't miss the flash of hurt in his eyes, and I felt a moment of guilt, but forced myself to swallow it down. This wasn't about him. Shit, it wasn't even about me. It was about Tillie and making sure she was safe. Protected. Loved. *Wanted.*

"Tillie, how would you like some ice cream?" Sadie spoke up and Tillie nodded frantically at the mention of her favorite treat. I knew I should protest Tillie having sweets that early but didn't. "If it's okay with you, I'd like to talk to your mommy for a minute, but I know that Aiden and Micah love ice cream, and I was kinda hoping you could go with them and keep them company."

Tillie glanced at me with a genuine smile on her face but before I could give permission, Aiden broke into the short-lived silence.

"I'm not leaving."

"Yes, Aiden, you are." There was no room for argument when a woman used that tone of voice. That I'm-a-mother-so-don't-argue tone. "Trust me, okay," she added, a little gentler.

When Aiden sighed with resignation and stood, setting Tillie on her feet, I made a mental note to ask Sadie how she did that. I could do it with Tillie but had never mastered the ability to use my mom-voice with an adult.

"Ice cweam!" Tillie bounced up and down, excitement overshadowing any fear she'd been experiencing a few moments before.

"This isn't over, sugar." Aiden leaned down and whispered in my ear before brushing a kiss on my temple and then disappearing with Tillie and Micah.

The breath I'd been holding the second I realized Aiden was coming closer to me rushed past my lips and my body deflated.

"They can be a bit much, huh?"

I'd forgotten Sadie was there until she spoke. I glanced at her and nodded. "Yeah, he can." Only after the words left my mouth did I realize that she'd been talking about *both* Micah and Aiden. *Shit.*

"Do you mind if I sit?" She pointed to the chair that Aiden had vacated.

Did I mind? *Yes.* Would I actually tell her that? *Not a chance.*

"Suit yourself."

She did exactly that and plopped down in the chair. "Tillie's beautiful."

"Thank you." I had no idea where this was going.

"Micah and I have two kids. Twins. Isaiah and Isabelle. They're Tillie's age."

"I don't mean to be rude, but where are you going with this?" I wasn't normally that bitchy, but I was tired and in pain. And not in the mood for conversation.

"I met Aiden not long after Micah found me in a field. I'd just escaped my abusive husband and wrecked the car once the adrenaline from fleeing wore off."

If she thought giving me a speech about how Aiden was a good man and I could trust him with Tillie was necessary, she could save it. That was not something I didn't already know. I trusted him more than anyone else in the world, but he was not who I was worried about. When I didn't speak for a few minutes, Sadie continued.

"It took me a long time to get past what was done to me." She gave a nervous chuckle and waved her hand back and forth as if to say whatever she'd been through hadn't been a big deal. "Micah was there every step of the way. As was everyone else in the BRB. Including Aiden."

"Why are you telling me all of this?"

"Because I want you to know you aren't alone. I want you to know that I've been where you're at. Maybe not *exactly*, but I get it." She slowly lifted the hem of her shirt to expose a jagged scar right above her belly button. "Serrated knife, courtesy of my ex."

I couldn't tear my eyes away from the puckered flesh. It was so much more than just a scar. I should know. It was a battle scar. A reminder that she'd suffered. But also a reminder that she'd survived.

"I can see that that got your attention." Her voice broke through the haze of thoughts, memories. She let her shirt drop, hiding her warrior patch from me and breaking the spell. "You can talk to me and I won't judge. You're not alone anymore."

"I know Aiden won't hurt me." That was the only thing that came to mind. "And I know he wouldn't hurt Tillie either."

"Why didn't you tell him about Tillie?" Ah, there it was. The question that no doubt had been hovering on the tip of her tongue that whole time.

My defenses sprang into place, and while the mental barrier kept others out, it didn't keep my anger from escaping. "How is that any of your business?"

"I suppose it's not." She was unruffled by my question. "But Aiden's important to me. If you don't want to talk to me, that's fine, but I won't sit back and watch him get hurt in the process of you healing."

Despite her threatening tone, I still felt no judgment from her. Just simple fact. An image of her scar entered my mind, and I reminded myself that she might be the one person who could understand. And if she wasn't that person then I'd run… again.

"It's complicated." I'd made up my mind to talk to her, tell her why I'd left, but that didn't mean it was going to be easy.

"Scarlett, of course it's complicated. Life's complicated."

"When I found out I was pregnant, I didn't know what to do. I barely knew Aiden. I mean, I thought I loved him, but did I really know him?" I prayed that would be enough of an explanation, even as my gut screamed that it wasn't an explanation at all.

"Okay. I get that but, how come you didn't tell him?"

Shame-infused heat flooded my cheeks. The truth was not flattering, and I didn't want to give her any reason to dislike me, but if I was going to need her help, Aiden's help, I owed them some sort of explanation.

"I, um, wanted security, ya know?"

"And?"

"I just felt like my best option at that point was my ex." I knew how bad that sounded and now I knew how stupid it was, but at the time, it seemed like the *only* option.

"You mean your stalker?" Clearly it sounded as bad as I thought.

I fidgeted with the blanket before answering. "Yes," I mumbled, unable to meet her eyes.

"Look, Scarlett, I'm not judging. Just trying to understand." Her tone was soft, reassuring.

I raised my head and finally met her stare. "At the time, Justin had found me and kept telling me how much he loved me. I believed him. And a part of me still loved him. Like I said, I barely knew Aiden, I was twenty-three and pregnant. I went with what I thought made the most sense. I was wrong."

"Were you afraid of Aiden? Of his reaction?"

"No. Yes. I don't know." I thought back to the moment I'd

seen the little pink lines pop up on the test. I'd been shocked, scared… stupid.

"Was Justin the one that did this to you?" Her hand swept in the direction of my body to indicate my numerous injuries.

I nodded, not trusting my voice.

"Has he done this before?" Her hand rested over mine on the mattress in a comforting gesture.

I shook my head. "Nothing this bad. We haven't been together in a long time, but he's never left us alone." The conversation took a toll on me, and I really wanted the first person to hear the details to be Aiden, so I didn't elaborate.

I tried to stifle a yawn but was unsuccessful.

"You're getting tired. Why don't you rest and we can bring Tillie back tomorrow if you're feeling up to it."

"I need to see her before you leave." Panic at the thought of not seeing my daughter again had the monitors beeping at a rapid pace and served to keep me awake.

"Calm down, Scarlett. We won't leave without you seeing Tillie." Sadie had stood and moved her hand from mine to my shoulder. Her gesture had the intended effect, and the staccato rhythm of the machines normalized as the pressure in my chest eased.

"She likes to be read to when she goes to bed." The words were clipped, but only because I was fighting like hell to not completely shatter. I was Tillie's mother. I should be reading her bedtime stories. But I couldn't.

"Does she have a favorite?" Sadie seemed to understand, and I was grateful when she went with the new direction in the conversation.

"She likes The Giant Jam Sandwich." I'd read that book to her so many times that the pages were becoming tattered.

"I'll make sure to pick it up at the store. Is there anything else I should know?"

"She wets the bed sometimes. Not every night," I rushed to add, "but maybe once a week or so."

"That's not a problem. We'll make sure we have a mattress protector. Anything else? Favorite foods? Allergies?"

"She loves peanut butter and jelly. Strawberry jelly. She'll refuse to eat it if it's grape jelly. And she's allergic to cats."

"Okay, I'll stock up on PB&J stuff. She's not allergic to dogs, is she?" Sadie looked concerned as she asked that.

"No. She'll be fine with Aiden's dogs." I remembered that Aiden trained dogs and instantly felt better about Tillie being in his home. "Is Sully still around?" I glanced at Sadie expectantly.

"Oh, yes. He's a sweetheart, and very protective. He's getting older, but still around."

"I remember him making me feel safe." At first, he'd been just a big scary Boxer but after a while, he'd wormed his way into my heart. Just like his master.

"He is good at that." Sadie chuckled before she pulled out her phone. I watched as her fingers flew over the screen. "I'm letting them know they can come back." She held the screen for me to see after she was done.

"Okay."

No more than three or four minutes later, Tillie ran through the door with Aiden and Micah on her heels. Micah was smiling but Aiden looked… shell-shocked.

"Mommy! I gots to eat chocolate ice cweam. It was weally good." The evidence of her treat was all around her mouth, and I couldn't help but laugh.

"I see that, baby. Why don't you run to the bathroom and wash up?" I pointed to the door that stood ajar across the room.

"Come on, Tillie. I'll help." Sadie grasped Tillie's hand and took her into the bathroom to help her get clean.

"I has to pee." Tillie's voice drifted further away as they strode into the restroom and closed the door behind them.

Tension filled the room as soon as the latch clicked into place. I stared at Aiden and he relentlessly stared back. Micah, however, walked to the window and pretended interest in the brick wall that made up my view. Finally, I couldn't take the intensity and broke my gaze away to stare at the bed.

"I gave instructions to Sadie about Tillie." I was fidgeting with the blanket, not looking at him while I spoke. His shadow fell across the bed and still, I didn't look up.

"Look at me," he commanded.

I shook my head.

"Look. At. Me."

My eyes peered up at him, but I still didn't raise my head fully. He blew out a frustrated breath before his fingers lightly gripped my chin, forcing my head up.

"I'm not going to ask any more questions right now. I know you're tired, and I know you need to rest more than I need answers. But we will talk about this, sugar. Understand?" The anger from before was gone, replaced by determination.

Incapable of speech, I nodded. The moment his fingers touched skin, my body had ignited. He'd always had that effect on me. A single touch would have me melting into a horny puddle and only he held the key to turning the puddle into something solid.

His pupils dilated and his nostrils flared. No doubt he knew how my body was responding.

The sound of the bathroom door opening had Aiden dropping his hand and whipping around.

Tillie ran up to the bed and tried to jump up. She was too short, of course, but that didn't stop her from trying.

Aiden recovered from the interruption and turned to

scoop Tillie up in his arms. She shrieked, and his eyes grew comically round before he set her back down.

"I'm sorry. I didn't... I wasn't... shit." Aiden thrust a shaky hand through his hair.

"You said a bad word," Tillie said accusingly. "Mommy, tell him. Shit is a bad word."

"Tillie's right." I was struggling to hold back a laugh at the look on Aiden's face. "That's a dollar for the jar."

"You gots to pay the jar." Tillie tilted her head to look up at him. "Mommy says." Her hands were now on her hips mimicking a pose she'd seen from me many times.

Aiden dug out his wallet and pulled a dollar from it, handing it to Tillie. "Tuck it in your pocket and we'll put it in a jar when we get home."

"'Kay." She did what she was told before returning her attention to me.

"Baby, mommy's getting very sleepy." At that moment, a yawn escaped. "I think it's time that you went home with Aiden and got settled." It broke my heart to say those words, but I knew I couldn't hold on much longer.

"Peanut, your mommy's right. She needs her rest." Aiden placed his hand on Tillie's head and while she flinched, she didn't pull away from him. "Besides, we have to stop at the store on the way home so you can pick out a few toys."

Bribery? He was learning fast.

"How many toys can I get?" Tillie asked.

"Tillie!" I scolded. "That's not polite. Say you're sorry for the rude question."

Tillie's eyes flooded at my sharp tone, but I'd learned long ago how to deflect that look.

When she realized I wasn't backing down, she mumbled, "Sowwy."

"It's okay, peanut." I rolled my eyes at his response. Not

even a full twenty-four hours and he was already undermining my authority.

Ever resilient, Tillie moved on to the next topic. "I come see you every day." Tillie glanced at me and then to Aiden, simultaneously promising me that she *would* be in every day and challenging him to argue the point.

"Peanut, we'll come as many days as we can." Aiden was clever. He didn't outright *deny* her what she wanted, but left room for interpretation. Maybe he *would* get a handle on this parenting thing.

"Well, mommy, we gots to go." Tillie laid her head on the side of the bed. "I wuv you, mommy."

"I love you too, baby." I blew her a kiss and couldn't control the flow of tears as I watched her walk to the door.

"We'll come by tomorrow." Aiden's eyes held none of the heat that was there earlier. "She'll be fine, sugar." I nodded, unable to speak. "Get some rest. Before you know it, you'll be coming home with Scarlett and me." He kissed my forehead before turning on his heel and walking out of the room with the others.

I thought back over his words. *Before you know it, you'll be coming home with Scarlett and me.* He had no idea what bringing me home with him would mean. But even worse, he had no clue how much I wanted that to be true.

7

AIDEN

"Tillie, I said 'no.'"

I was quickly learning that Tillie was not always the sweet little girl I'd thought she was. We'd been in the toy store for almost two hours, and she was in the middle of her second temper tantrum because I wouldn't let her get a toy that was clearly too old for her. It even said so on the damn box.

"Aiden, just pick her up and let's go." Micah's voice was laced with frustration.

Sadie had gone home ahead of us to get a room ready for Tillie. At that moment, I was really wishing Micah and I hadn't insisted we'd be fine.

I didn't want to follow Micah's instruction because I was too worried about scaring her and causing even more narrowed suspicion-filled stares from the other shoppers. Whether their ogling was because of our imposing appearance or the way Tillie was acting, I had no idea. It didn't really matter, either.

I realized that I'd have to chance it and bent to scoop the screaming child into my arms. I tried to dodge her flailing arms, but I wasn't fast enough. She caught me in the cheek with a tiny fist and damn if it didn't actually smart a little. "Ouch," I roared.

Tillie immediately stilled and stared at me with wide eyes. Anger turned to fear, and she tucked her head into my shoulder and started crying.

"Peanut, I'm sorry. I didn't mean to yell." I cradled her trembling body and rubbed a hand up and down her back. "Shh, don't cry. I'm sorry." I glanced at Micah, only to see him fighting a grin. *Bastard.*

Apparently, sympathy took over because he sobered and walked toward us, shaking his head the entire time. "Munchkin, look at me," he said when he was close enough to put his hand on her back. His tone was commanding, as if Tillie were one of his subordinates, and I had to force myself not to react to it.

Tillie's crying slowed to a wet hiccup, and she lifted her head and twisted in my arms to look at him. My shirt was damp and clung to my skin. For a moment, I hadn't cared, but then I'd caught sight of her runny nose and realized it was likely a mixture of tears *and* snot. *Gross.*

"You hurt him." Micah pointed to my cheek but never took his gaze off of Tillie. "What do you say?"

Tillie's gaze followed his finger before she reached out with her own unsteady hand and inadvertently poked me in the eye. I winced, but otherwise didn't react. "Owie."

"Yes, owie," I said.

"Sowwy." She dropped her head to her chest but quickly snapped her head back up to look at me. "Do you need to west like mommy?"

Well, shit.

"No, peanut. I'll be okay." Just a little more colorful.

"'Kay." She rested her head on my shoulder and rubbed her eyes with her clenched fist. The events of the day, and likely her life, were catching up to her. She yawned and struggled to keep her eyes open.

"Go ahead and go to sleep, peanut. I'll wake you up when we get home." Home. The word held new meaning now. Before I knew it, her breathing evened out, and her body fully relaxed.

"That was fun," Micah said.

"Asshole." I tried to glare at him but ended up chuckling instead. "Push the damn cart so we can get the hell out of here. I'm starting to feel like a bug being inspected under a microscope." I scanned the space around us and realized that no one was staring any longer.

"You're really going to have to watch your language." He tipped his head to indicate the sleeping child in my arms. "She'll repeat everything she hears." As if I already forgot about the 'jar', he continued. "And you'll go broke."

I flipped him off. He was one to talk. I'd been shocked when his kids' first words hadn't been 'fuck', 'shit', and 'damn'.

After paying for the cartful of toys, we headed to the Jeep, and I put Tillie in the car seat. She stirred but didn't wake. It took me a solid ten minutes to buckle her in, and no doubt her ears would have burned if she'd heard what had been spewing from my mouth. Micah could have helped, but he hadn't. Instead, he stood back and watched me struggle, clearly enjoying the show.

As Micah drove us home, I sat sideways in the passenger seat so I could watch Tillie.

"She's not going anywhere."

"I know," I said, never taking my eyes off of her.

"Surreal, isn't it?"

"Is this how it's supposed to feel?" I asked, absently rubbing my hand over my chest.

"Like your heart's going to explode, it's so full?"

"Yeah."

"Exactly like." He nodded with a grin on his face.

"How do you make it stop?" I straightened in my seat to face forward.

"You don't." He glanced at me for a second before returning his concentration to the road. "Is that what you want? To make it stop."

I thought for a moment before responding. "No."

"I can turn around an—"

"I said, 'no,'" I snapped. Switching gears, I said, "Did you talk to anyone besides Sadie?" He nodded. "What'd they say?"

"They were surprised." He shrugged. "Happy for you, though. And they all *really* want to meet Tillie."

"Micah?" I took a deep breath and blew it out. "I really am sorry."

"Stop," he ordered. "Nothing to be sorry for. I thought we covered this." He really had mellowed with the addition of Sadie and the twins.

"Yeah. Yeah, we did. Doesn't change the fact that I fucked up." I was happy about Tillie. Really, I was. But that didn't make me less sorry for betraying my team. My family.

"Enough." He glanced in the rearview mirror, and his eyes narrowed.

I turned to see what he was looking at, and fury heated my blood. "Pull over."

"Aiden, this isn't the time or place."

"I don't fucking care. Pull. Over." I gritted my teeth against the rage.

Micah sighed and eased the Jeep to the shoulder of the road before cutting the engine. He glanced in the mirror again and then at me. "Don't do anything stupid."

"I won't." I was out of the vehicle and slamming my door before the words were even out of my mouth. I had a brief thought that I hoped it wouldn't wake Tillie, but it quickly fled as I turned and saw the source of my anger getting out of his car.

I fumed as he nonchalantly sauntered toward me, arms crossed over his chest, eyes hidden behind mirrored shades. I stomped toward him, hauled my arm back, and watched my fist connect with Jackson's jaw.

"Shit," he muttered as he cupped his face. "I should arrest your ass."

"Why the fuck are you following us?" My chest heaved and I itched to punch him again. All of the anger from my day was bubbling over, and Jackson's face was as good a target as any.

"I wasn't following you." He thrust his fingers through his hair and blew out a breath. "I was headed to your place."

"Why?" Jackson had never given me reason to not trust him before, but now? I hadn't been his first phone call when he'd found out about Scarlett and Tillie. After all the BRB had been through, I'd trusted him. And now he owed me an explanation before I would even entertain the thought of trusting him again.

"Because there's an ongoing investigation into what happened with Scarlett, and I wanted to talk to you about it." His eyes met mine. "See if you could shed some light on the situation."

"Fuck you." I jabbed a finger at his chest. "You should have called me the second you knew it was Scarlett."

"I know you guys like to pretend otherwise, but I still have a job to do. And guess what?" He crossed his arms over his chest. "Nowhere in my job description does it require me to notify you of every investigation I'm involved in."

He may have been right, but it did little to ease my anger. "You knew I was looking for her. You fucking knew."

"Yes, I knew." He sighed and dropped his arms to his sides. "Doesn't change the facts. I have a job to do."

"Fuck your job. I'm a father now and somehow—"

"So am I!" He raged.

That shut me up, and my body deflated as the anger fled. I turned from him, unable to bear witness to the emotions crossing his features. Anger, sadness, *guilt*.

I heard gravel crunching and whirled around when I heard Jackson scream. Not a girly scream. No, it was a deep, guttural scream that tore out of him and echoed in the air around us. Both of his fists came down on the hood of his patrol car, leaving dents in their wake.

Afterward, he backed up a few steps and stared at the damage. He turned toward me before hanging his head. When he glanced back up, his face was devoid of any emotion.

"I'll see you both later." He looked over my shoulder, and when I followed his gaze, I saw Micah standing behind me. With that, he got in his car and peeled out, gravel spraying as he went.

"What the hell was that about?" I scrubbed my hands over my face before facing Micah.

"No clue." Micah shook his head. "Come on." He got back in the Jeep, but I hesitated. I squinted at the road before us, the one Jackson had just fled on. I could no longer see his vehicle, but a slimy film coated my soul as his words replayed in my head. *So am I.*

What the hell?

I shook off the thought and forced myself to get in the Jeep. I glanced at Tillie, thankful she appeared to still be sleeping peacefully. I had to focus on her now. Not Jackson's problems. Or his betrayal.

That could wait for another day.

When Micah parked in front of my cabin, I didn't budge. I sat and stared out the window. It had only been several hours, but it felt like a lifetime had passed since I'd peeled out on my bike and headed for the hospital. At the time, I'd had no fucking clue that I'd be bringing someone home. Certainly not a child. *My* child.

"You gonna sit here long?" Micah asked.

I turned from the window to look at him.

"I don't know what the fuck I'm doing." Everything came crashing down on me at once. "I can't be a dad. Shit, I don't even have one. I have no clue what it takes to be a good father."

"Do you think I'm a good father to my children?" Micah's question made no sense. This wasn't about him. It was about me.

"Of course you're a good father."

"Then follow my example." He made it sound so easy. I had a feeling that nothing about this situation was going to be easy. "You might not have had an example of what it takes when you were growing up, but you do now. I'm not perfect, but guess what?"

"What?"

"You don't have to be perfect. That little girl," he said as he hitched his thumb over his shoulder to indicate Tillie. "She's not going to give a rat's ass about perfect. She's just going to want your time and attention and love. Give her that and you'll do just fine."

I blew out a breath and considered his words. Sure, I hadn't had a father figure growing up. Not one that gave two shits about me and certainly not one that had loved me. When I think about what I wish I'd had throughout my childhood, the one consistent theme in all of it was attention... love. Micah was right.

"Mommy?" Tillie's voice pulled me the rest of the way out of the dark hole I'd mentally buried myself in.

I forced a smile and turned in my seat. "Hey, peanut. Did you have a good nap?"

I heard Micah mutter 'oh shit' at the same time Tillie said, "I don't take naps." I watched as she crossed her little arms over her chest and jutted her chin. "I not a baby."

"Okay, peanut." I looked to Micah for some guidance, or at the very least, some brotherly commiseration. When all I saw was him trying, *hard*, not to laugh and holding his hands up in a don't-look-at-me gesture, I returned my attention to my daughter. "You ready to go inside?"

She glared at me for another few seconds before peering out the window. Her eyes widened when they landed on the cabin, and I squinted at the structure, trying to see what she saw. She pointed at it and asked, "Is that yours?"

I couldn't help the chuckle that escaped. "Well, peanut, yeah. But it's yours now too." I opened my door and stepped out, breathing in the crisp air.

As I turned to get Tillie out of the back seat, I heard the familiar sound of my front door opening. I glanced over my shoulder and saw Brie and Sadie coming out of my cabin, trash bags in their hands.

"Uh, what's all this about?" My gaze went back and forth between the women and Micah.

"You didn't seriously think we were going to let you bring a child home to whatever debauchery goes on here, did you?" Brie's eyes danced with laughter as she jogged down the steps and toward the trash bin to deposit her bag.

"Well, no, I—"

"We heard that *woman* peel out of here this morning." Brie smiled to soften her words. After throwing her trash away, she came right up to me and stopped.

"What?" I snapped, a little more harshly than I'd intended.

They were pointing out things that I hadn't even thought about, and it made me feel like an idiot. Not that they weren't right. The condition of my home had been no place for a little girl. But I should have thought about it first.

Sadie came to stand next to Brie. "Welcome to the club." She wrapped her arms around my waist and gave me a hug. I relaxed into her hold and hugged her back. "You're going to be a great father, Aiden."

"Thanks, Red." The nickname she'd had since the night Micah found her slipped out. I took a step back and caught Micah glaring at me. He was so territorial, regardless of who it was near his wife.

Chuckling, I turned and opened the back door and leaned in to get Tillie out of the car seat. "Come on, peanut."

She wrapped her arms around my neck and let me lift her from the car but squirmed to be put down as soon as she was clear of the door.

"Sadie!" Tillie squealed when she was on her feet and threw her arms around Sadie's legs.

"Hi munchkin." Sadie chuckled at Tillie's exuberance. She knelt down and grabbed Tillie's hands in hers. "Can I introduce you to my friend?" She asked, pointing to Brie.

Tillie bobbed her head up and down with excitement.

"Her name is Brie. Can you say 'hi'?"

"Hi." She waved her tiny hand at Brie. "I'm Tillie."

"It's nice to meet you, Tillie." Brie gave Tillie her friendliest smile and winked. "I'm a friend of your da... er, Aiden's." She met my eyes after her slip up, and I simply shrugged. I had no idea if I should be called 'daddy' to Tillie or not. Just because I was biologically, didn't mean she was ready for that. Or that I was.

"Do you have kids for me to pway wif?"

"I'm afraid I don't."

"Oh. Well, maybe we can still pway together." Tillie put

her fist on her hip and appeared to be in deep thought about whether or not it was acceptable to play with an adult.

"I'd like that. You name the time and place, and I'll be there." Brie ruffled Tillie's hair and then stood, while Tillie looked at me expectantly.

"Maybe tomorrow you can get together and play with Isabelle and Isaiah, and if Brie wants to play too, she can. Would you like that?"

Tillie stood still for a moment before slowly nodding her head.

"What time works for you all?" I asked, glancing from Brie to Sadie and then to Micah.

"How about nine tomorrow morning? I can either bring the kids here or come pick Tillie up, and they can all play at our place." Sadie was the one who responded.

"Nine is fine. And how about you pick Tillie up, and they can play at your place? Give me a chance to do some… work." I really wanted to start digging into the only information I had from when Scarlett was here four years ago.

"Sounds like a plan." With that, Sadie turned and walked to Micah, throwing her arms around him for a hug.

He bent over and kissed the top of her head, and jealousy shot through me. Would I ever have that? A connection to a woman that was like life or death? A relationship with the mother of my child? In that moment, it hit me hard just how much I wanted it.

"Aiden," Brie said as she stepped up to me. "Griffin said he'd stop by when he got home from his case."

"Right." In the craziness of the day, I'd forgotten he'd been working a new case involving a woman with two children who were running from a crazy ex.

"Also, there's food in the fridge." She looked down at Tillie and winked. "And there might be ice cream in the freezer."

"Ice cweam!" Tillie cheered.

"Mint chocolate chip, I think." Brie bent back down so she was eye-level with Tillie. "I think there's also a princess bed and some princess clothes." Tillie smiled. "I mean, if you know a little girl who might like those things."

"I'm a wittle girl." Tillie stepped closer to Brie. "I wanna be a princess."

Brie's gaze lifted to mine and she smiled. She'd always had a way with kids. She was the fun 'aunt' and something told me she'd have no problems with Tillie. "Then I think you should go inside and have a look around."

"'Kay." Tillie grabbed the hem of my shirt and tugged. "C'mon."

"Thank you," I whispered to Brie.

"No problem." She stood on her tiptoes and wrapped her arms around my neck. "Go get to know your little girl," she whispered in my ear before kissing me on the cheek and stepping back and looking back down at my daughter. "It was nice to meet you, Tillie. I'll see you tomorrow."

"Aiden, I'll help you carry everything inside, and then I'm heading out." Micah spoke up for the first time since we got out of the car. "You gonna be good?"

"Yeah, man. I'm good." I really believed that. I might not have everything figured out yet, but surely I could handle things for one night.

8

AIDEN

I bolted upright as a scream pierced the air. I immediately reached for the gun in my nightstand and let the weight of it settle my racing heart. I threw off the sheet and swung my legs over the edge of the bed, grabbing my cell phone as I did. Another scream hit me, and that's when I remembered Tillie was in the cabin.

I tore out of the bedroom, hell-bent on protecting Tillie from whatever was scaring her. I reached her bedroom door at the end of the hallway and threw it open, drawing my gun. Based on her screams, I was sure I'd be putting a bullet in some asshole's head, so I was shocked to see her in her room, *alone*, twisting and turning in the sheets of her brand new princess 'big girl bed'.

I tucked the gun in the back of the waistband of my boxer briefs, silently thanking God that I hadn't slept naked like I normally do. I was at her bedside in three long strides. Her eyes were squeezed tightly shut, and her face was scrunched up.

"Tillie?" I gently shook her by the shoulder, trying to get

her to wake up while simultaneously afraid to spook her. "Hey, hey, hey, peanut. It's okay."

She continued to toss and turn and mumble incoherent words. I shook her a little harder, and her eyes flew open as she threw her arms up and shrank into the bed.

"Whoa." I put my hands up in a gesture of surrender. I didn't want to scare her more than she already was. Her eyes widened, but when recognition hit, her body relaxed slightly, and she sat up a little. "Were you having a bad dream, peanut?"

She nodded and looked toward the door before returning her gaze to me. "He was here."

She'd been asleep when I'd stormed in, so I knew she hadn't seen anyone. At least not anywhere other than in her nightmare. I didn't say that, though.

"Who was here?"

"My other daddy."

Tension coiled and it took everything in me not to react. "What was he doing?"

"Where's Mommy?" Tillie rubbed her eyes and looked around the room, fear clear in her expression.

"Aw, peanut, remember? Mommy's resting at the hospital." I reached out to tuck a strand of hair behind her ear, and when she flinched, my heart cracked. "Can you tell me what happened in your dream?" I knew a lot about nightmares. Had up close and personal experience with them, and if her screams were any indication, she was suffering from PTSD and I needed to know what caused it if I was going to help her.

Tillie looked at me for several minutes, her eyes narrowing as if she was trying to decide whether or not she could trust me. She could, without question, but she had to learn that on her own.

She glanced at the door and then back to me. "He was mad at Mommy."

"Do you know what he was mad about?" It took everything in me to keep my voice calm and even when all I wanted to do was rage and beat the shit out of someone.

She shook her head. "I want Sadie."

"Okay, peanut. I'll text her." I sent off a quick message to Sadie, feeling horrible about waking her up, but not horrible enough not to. I watched my phone for her response, and when it came, my breath whooshed out of me. I hadn't even realized I'd been holding it. "She's on her way."

"'Kay.'" Tillie sniffled and my heart cracked a bit more. How the hell did Scarlett do this?

We sat there, with nothing but the sound of my racing heart and Tillie's sniffles to fill the silence. Tillie had a deer in the headlights look in her eyes, constantly glancing from me to the door and back again. After a very tense few minutes, the sound of an engine reached my ears, and I jumped up to go let Sadie in.

"I'll be right back, peanut. I'm gonna let her in." Tillie shrank back into the bed and pulled the covers up over her head.

Not wanting to leave her alone when she was scared, I froze for several seconds, agonizing over what to do. Mind made up, I ran to the front door and threw it open and jogged back to the bedroom. I wasn't gone for more than twenty seconds. Tillie was still under the blanket and it was shaking, telling me she was too.

"I'm back, peanut." Again, I kept my voice low, so as not to startle her.

The pink comforter, with some Disney princess on it, lowered and Tillie peered over the top, knuckles white from the grip she had on it. "Where is she?"

"I'm right here," Sadie's sunny voice saved me from

answering as she breezed through the doorway. When she reached the bed, she sat down and looked at my daughter. "Hi, sweetie."

"Hi." Tillie took in Sadie and then she glanced at me before ducking her head.

Sadie's gaze followed Tillie's to me, and she gave a sad smile. "Aiden, can I get a few minutes alone with Tillie?"

"Oh, uh, sure." I thrust a shaky hand through my hair. "I'll be in the living room if you guys need me."

"Thanks, Aiden." Again, Sadie had that sad smile.

I took one last look at my daughter before backing out of the room and pulling the door closed. Just before the latch engaged, I stopped and pushed it back open a crack. It might not have been the best idea I'd ever had, but I wanted to hear what was said.

For the first few minutes, I didn't hear much. Sadie was talking so low that it was hard to make out her words, and Tillie's voice was so soft that it was equally hard. Soon, their voices rose and I picked up bits and pieces of the conversation. Something about a man getting angry with Scarlett and Tillie begging him to stop.

Motherfucker!

"Has this happened before?" Sadie asked her.

When I didn't hear a response, I tried to peek in the crack of the door, but I couldn't see anything.

"Did he ever hurt you?" Another question from Sadie.

"Sometimes, when mommy wasn't around."

That was one answer I wish I hadn't heard. My fists balled at my sides, and I turned away from the door, intent on punching a hole in the wall. I managed to stop myself, barely. The only thing that kept me in check was not wanting to scare an already terrified little girl even more.

I forced myself back to the crack in the door, leaning against the wall so my ear was right next to it.

"Aw, sweetie. I'm sorry." Sadie's tone was soothing, and I imagined she was hugging Tillie. I'd seen her do that countless times with her own kids, and it always seemed to help.

Emotion overwhelmed me at the thought. *I* wanted to be the one hugging Tillie. *I* wanted to be the one my daughter went to for comfort.

You will be. It's just going to take time.

How much time?

Too much.

I need her to trust—

"How much did you hear?" Sadie's question stopped the internal debate in its tracks. I hadn't even heard her walk out of the room. Some Navy Seal I was.

"Enough."

"Aiden, this isn't your fault." Sadie's hand rested on my forearm.

"I could've protected them." Fury settled in my gut like a brick. "Why the fuck—"

"Stop." She silenced me with a hand over my mouth.

My eyes widened at her action. Not many people would dare to order me around when I was angry, let alone touch me, but not this little red-headed spitfire. I gave a slight nod of my head.

"Let's go into the other room and talk. She finally fell asleep, and I don't want to wake her." Sadie removed her hand and walked away from me, not looking to see if I followed. She knew I would.

When we were both in the living room, Sadie sat on the couch and I paced. I was glad I didn't have carpet because I'd likely wear a hole in it.

"Aiden, sit down."

I glanced at her but didn't sit. It was like I was afraid that if I sat down, I was somehow giving up. And I refused to give up.

"Please." Her voice softened but still held a hint of authority.

"I can't." I stopped pacing and looked at her.

"Why not?" She tilted her head as she looked at me.

"Because if I do…"

"Aiden?" The softness was gone and back was full-on mom-voice.

"Hmm?" Rather than look at her anymore, my head dropped and I stared at the floor.

"This isn't your fault. And sitting down doesn't change that. No one thinks you're going to give up."

My head snapped up and our eyes locked. I knew the look on my face had to register my surprise at her accuracy. "How'd you—"

She threw her head back and laughed, cutting me off. When the hilarity subsided, she shook her head. "You're forgetting who I'm married to."

"Right." A chuckle escaped me. "How do you stand it?"

"I love him," she said simply, as if that explained everything. Hell, maybe it did. "He's a good man, a good father and all of you are just alike. You get so in your head sometimes that you can't see what's right in front of your face."

"And what's that?"

"You can't save everyone. And the fate of the entire world does not rest on your shoulders. You have people who love you and will have your back. Every time. But, sometimes there simply isn't anything you could have done to stop bad things from happening."

"Okay, Red. When did you get so smart?" I ducked the pillow that was thrown at my head. I held my hands up in surrender before finally giving up the fight and sitting on the couch next to her. "Seriously. You make it sound so simple. But it's not."

"No, it's not. But not much ever is. At least, not anything

worth it." She yawned and I glanced at the clock. Three in the morning. She had to be exhausted. Not only had she come over to help, no questions asked, but she also had her own twins to care for.

"Why don't you head home? We can talk more later."

"I'll head home in a few. There are some things that we need to talk about."

"Okay." I drew the word out to where it almost sounded like a question.

"Aiden, how much do you know about what brought Scarlett here four years ago?"

Caught off guard by the question, I sat back and thought about the day Scarlett showed up on my doorstep. Thought about the things she'd revealed while she was here. Frustration hummed in my veins as I realized I didn't know shit. Not anything major anyway.

"Not much. She claimed she had a stalker." Leaning forward, I rested my elbows on my knees. My eyes narrowed as I thought harder. "She never did give me a name."

"Justin."

My head swiveled so fast, it made me dizzy. "Who the fuck is Justin?"

"According to her, her ex, her stalker, and the one responsible for her injuries, all rolled into one neat little package." When my mouth opened to interrupt, she held up her hand. "I didn't get much more than that. But based on what she did say and what I know about these types of situations, I'd bet my last dollar that Justin has been tormenting her for years."

"But you don't know for sure?"

"No, I don't."

I hopped up and started pacing again. Anger burned like acid in my veins. After several furious paths across the room, I came to a stop in front of Sadie and pulled my phone from my pocket.

"What are you doing?" she asked.

Not even bothering to look at her, I mumbled, "Texting Micah. He's going to want to hear everything and I need his help."

The device was snatched from my hand, forcing a growl from my throat. I glared at Sadie, who stood in front of me with a scowl on her face. "What are *you* doing?"

"You are not texting my husband." She tossed my cell on the couch, and when I went to step around her, she blocked my path and put a restraining hand on my chest. "Aiden, no. He's got the twins so I can be here. Besides, it's the middle of the night. There is nothing anyone can do right now."

"Damnit." I blew out a frustrated breath, knowing she was right and hating it.

"Listen, we're both exhausted. You've had a long day. An emotional day. Why don't you get some sleep and I'll be back in the morning to pick Tillie up for that playdate?"

She stared at me, waiting for some type of response, and I gave her a tight nod. Apparently satisfied with that, she stood on her tiptoes and brushed a kiss across my cheek. "Love you, Aiden."

A smile tugged at the corners of my lips. "Love you too, Red."

With that, she turned to leave but something forced her back around. "Aiden? One more thing."

"Yeah?"

"Before we all talk, you really should get Scarlett's side of things. Not everything may be as it appears." Before I could question her, she had walked out the door and the sound of an engine reached through the open window.

Once I was alone, I dropped to the couch and propped my bare feet on the coffee table. I thought back through everything Scarlett had ever told me about her stalker. I thought about everything that had happened today. And I thought about the little girl in the other room. All of this brought on more questions than answers, so I gave in and stood, intent on going to bed to try to get a few hours of sleep.

On my way, I paused at the door to Tillie's room and peaked in at her. Satisfied that she was peacefully asleep, I trudged the rest of the way to my room, my mind swirling. I threw myself on my bed and tried to mentally shut down. After more stewing, there was only one clear thing I kept coming back to.

I needed to talk to Scarlett.

9

SCARLETT

"How'd you sleep?"

I rolled my eyes at the nurse. The third nurse that morning to ask me the same damn question.

"Fine," I mumbled. What I wanted to say was *'How the fuck do you think I slept?'*, but I kept my snarky thoughts to myself. I didn't want to piss off the people who could help me get out of here quicker. Get to Tillie faster.

"Oh, that's so good to hear." This nurse was older than the rest and actually really friendly, so I found my frustration dissipating the longer she was in the room. "The doctor says that you should be able to go home today, provided that there's someone there to help you."

My mind immediately conjured up an image of Aiden. He'd been coming to see me every day and every day he brought Tillie with him. I still wasn't used to the fact that Tillie was actually with her father, or that he even wanted to be in that role, but he'd said he did and I needed his help just a bit longer, so I hoped he was being honest.

"I have someone." I picked at the sheets, nervousness

seeping in at the thought of being with Aiden. In his home. Where Tillie was conceived.

"It wouldn't be a certain gentleman that's been spending a lot of his time here, now would it?" There was a rosy tint to the woman's cheeks, but I detected no malice. Most women were out to get the latest gossip, but she seemed genuinely interested. Or maybe I was just trying to justify my sudden desire to open up to her. She must have sensed my hesitation because she added, "Oh, honey. Never mind. It's none of my business. I just saw the way you both looked at each other. And, lord, the way he looks at that little girl. He'd walk through hell and back for both of you."

"I guess." What else could I say? All I saw from Aiden was anger and pain. And who could blame him?

"Well, enough of that." The entire time she'd been in the room, she'd been checking the machines, my vitals, anything and everything she could. Now, she set the chart on the table at the side of the bed, and really looked at me.

"What?" I snapped and then immediately wanted to call the word back. She was harmless, and there was no reason for me to take my unnamable emotions out on her.

"Hm, nothing." She turned toward the door, and once she reached the threshold, she pivoted back to face me. "You know, it's okay to rely on people every once in a while. Not everyone will hurt you the way *he* hurt you." Satisfied that she'd said what she wanted to say, she left the room.

And sometimes, you just have to accept that you're not built to love and be loved.

The doctor had just left my hospital room, after having declared me officially discharged. I'd texted Aiden earlier to let him know I would likely be released that day. He still wasn't there. To be fair, I hadn't actually asked him to pick me up. I hadn't been able to, but I'd assumed he'd somehow know that I'd need a ride.

Taking a deep breath, I picked up my cell phone, the one Aiden had gotten me the first week I'd been there and dialed his number.

"Hello?" His deep voice came through and heat shot straight to parts of me that I'd thought were long dead.

"Uh, hi. I was just… um… do you think…" What the hell was wrong with me? I'd never stammered around him. Or with anyone else for that matter.

"Is that mommy? Lemme talk to mommy." I heard my daughter's excitement in the background, and a smile bloomed.

"Peanut, you're going to see her in…"

The rest of his sentence went unheard as the phone went silent. At the same time the silence hit, Aiden and Tillie walked through the door. Well, Aiden walked. Tillie skipped.

"Sorry we're late. We would've been here sooner, but someone had to stop for balloons." Aiden had a rueful smile on his face as he tilted his head toward our daughter.

Tillie held long white strings, with 'Get Well' balloons attached to the end. How I'd missed that when she'd walked in, I had no idea.

No idea? Get real.

Okay, maybe Aiden's body had been a momentary distraction, but he was so damn sexy. And there was something about him that made everything else in the room disappear.

"It's uh, no big deal." The hunger I felt was mirrored in his eyes, and after a tense moment, he turned toward Tillie, breaking the spell.

"Hey, peanut. Why don't you give those to your mom."

Tillie shoved her clenched fist toward me. "Here, mommy. These are for you."

"Thank you, baby." I took the balloons from her, glancing around to see where I could put them. There weren't any options, so I held on to them. "I love them."

"Aiden says you're going to live at his house." As she talked, I didn't miss the hurt that crossed his face at Tillie calling him by his name.

"And how do you feel about that?" She seemed to have warmed up to him a little, but I was in the room. Every time I saw them together, I was in the room, so it was hard to tell if she really did trust him, or if she appeared to trust him because she felt safe with me.

Rather than answer, Tillie shrugged. She peered over her shoulder and up at Aiden. He smiled at her, but it didn't reach his eyes.

"Well, I for one, am excited." I injected some cheer into my voice, whether for Tillie's benefit, Aiden's or mine, I had no idea.

"You are?"

"Really?"

Both of them spoke at once, causing a laugh to erupt past my lips.

"Yes, really. It'll be an adventure. And I love adventures." That was a lie, but they didn't need to know that.

Aiden shoved his hands in his pockets and rocked back and forth on his heels. It was rare to see him uncomfortable or nervous, but he appeared so then.

"So, did the doctor give you instructions? Should I talk to him before we leave?"

"I've got it all here." I picked up the folder of papers the doctor left with me. "But if you want to talk to him, go ahead."

"Yeah, I think I will. Just to be sure." With that, he was gone.

I focused my attention on Tillie, who was quietly standing in front of me. I had changed into clothes that Aiden had brought me on an earlier visit and was sitting on the side of the bed. I decided to take advantage of this rare alone time with her.

"Baby, have you liked staying with Aiden?"

"Uh-huh. I was scared at first, but Auntie Sadie helped a lot."

Auntie Sadie?

"And I still get scared sometimes, but not always."

All of my motherly hackles rose and zeroed in on the fact that she still got scared at times. "What scares you, baby?"

She shrugged.

"Don't worry, mommy. I make sure I don't make him mad."

All air rushed from my body. Is that what she thought? That all it took was someone getting angry to do the things she's seen done to me?

You did this to her.

I told my internal self to shut the hell up and stared at Tillie. She stared back, a confused expression on her face.

"You 'kay, mommy?"

I snapped out of whatever daze I was in and thought about her question.

No.

I was not okay. But that wasn't something that needed to be shared with a four-year-old.

"Yeah, baby. Mommy's fine." I ran my fingers through her silky hair, savoring the feel, and forced a reassuring smile.

As nervous as I was to be in the same home with Aiden, I couldn't let Tillie see that. She needed to know that I felt safe if she was going to feel safe. Besides, my nervousness had nothing to do with fear that Aiden would hurt me or Tillie.

No. I was nervous because I knew that Aiden and I together were like fire and gasoline. Explosive.

10

AIDEN

"Welcome home."

I swept my gaze over the living room, trying to see it through Scarlett's eyes. I was nervous as hell to have her in my space. Stupid, really. It's not like she'd never been there before. She'd practically lived there, but this time it was different. This time I wanted to make sure she never left.

I glanced at her, and she appeared frozen in the doorway. Tillie stood at her side and held her hand. Normally Tillie would come through the door and rush to her toys, but not this time. This time it was like she sensed that Scarlett needed her to get through this. Whatever *this* was.

"Everything looks the same." There was wonder in her tone, and her shoulders slightly relaxed.

"Not what you were expecting?" I shoved my hands in my pockets, content to wait for her answer. She didn't make me wait long.

"No, it's not that. It's just…" She shrugged.

"Just what, sugar?"

"Mommy, can I go play?" Saved by Tillie. At least temporarily.

"Sure, baby. But maybe in a few minutes you can show me your room and all of your toys? I'd love to see them." Scarlett's smile was genuine as she gazed down into Tillie's eyes.

"'Kay".

Tillie took off like a shot toward her bedroom. Both Scarlett and I laughed at her, shaking our heads at her exuberance, but then our gazes caught. And held.

She was the first to break the spell.

"Aiden, thank—"

"Don't." My clipped tone conveyed my annoyance at her. "Don't thank me."

"But—"

"No, Scarlett. You don't need to thank me for taking care of *my* daughter."

Pain flashed in her eyes, and I reminded myself that she'd just gotten out of the hospital and probably needed some time to get settled in before I tried to have *that* conversation.

I turned on my heel and walked toward the kitchen, not bothering to see if she followed. I pulled some lunch meat out of the refrigerator for Scarlett and me and got the peanut butter out of the cupboard for Tillie's PB&J. Next on the list was the jelly and bread.

"What are you doing?" Scarlett spoke in a hushed tone, as if afraid to set off the ticking time bomb she thought I was.

"Making lunch. Tillie usually eats around this time, and I figure you're probably ready for something other than hospital food." I didn't look at her the entire time I spoke. I didn't trust myself to. One look at her and I'd do one of two things: rage at her or crumble at her feet. Neither was acceptable then.

"Oh. Is there anything I can do to help?"

"I got it." *Don't turn around. Don't react to the hurt in her voice.*

"Just let me hel—"

I slammed the knife down on the counter and whirled around. She'd had to keep talking. "Why the fuck did you keep her from me?"

She shrank back at my words and lowered her eyes to the floor. "Not now, Aiden. I'm too tired to have this conversation."

"Not now? You've got to be fucking kidding me!" I stalked toward her and got in her face. "She's my daughter. My daughter! This is a conversation we should have had, oh, I don't know, four years ago. I've waited long enough so don't pull this 'not now' bullshit."

"Aiden, you're scaring me." Her eyes were wide, giving credence to her statement.

I didn't care. I was pissed and I wanted answers.

"Answer me," I grated out through clenched teeth.

"I can't."

"Yes, you can. Answer. Me."

Tears gathered at the corners of her eyes, and when one escaped, my anger cooled. Unable to stand her sadness and knowing that I'd been a part of the cause, I did the only thing I could. Slammed my mouth down on hers in a bruising kiss.

At first, she was hesitant, but the prodding of my tongue forced her lips to part. I showed no mercy, thrusting my tongue between them and grasping the back of her head to pull her closer, as if that were possible. Her arms came around me, and she tugged me to her, aligning our bodies perfectly. Every single thought left me, replaced by scorching heat that seemed to burn me from the inside out.

When Scarlett moaned, I swallowed it down, straight to my cock. Her pebbled nipples grazed my chest, forcing a groan to escape. Just when I was about to lift her up and press her back against the wall, she tore her lips from mine. Her chest was heaving, her breaths were labored, but the fear was gone. Her eyes were pools of liquid fire, and I knew in that moment, that if she let me, I'd drown in them.

"Aiden." She shook her head and took a step back. "I can't… we shouldn't… I just can't." She turned on her heel and ran through the living room and out the front door.

I didn't follow. Not that I didn't have reason to think otherwise, but I was confident that she wouldn't actually leave. Not without Tillie.

Shoving my fingers through my hair, I drew in a shaky breath. I glanced at the clock and noticed it was now past lunchtime for Tillie, so I quickly finished cutting her sandwich into triangles, like she liked it, and tossed it on a paper plate. I set it on the table and then went to get her so she could eat.

"Peanut, lunch is ready." I leaned around the doorframe to look into her room and saw that she was curled up on her bed, surrounded by the many stuffed animals she'd accumulated over the last month, sound asleep.

I turned to leave and nearly had a heart attack when I came face to face with Scarlett, arms crossed over her chest.

"What are you doing?" she whispered.

Rather than answer, I grabbed her by the elbow and pulled her along beside me as I made my way to the kitchen. When we got there, she yanked her arm from my grasp and dropped it to her side.

"Nothing. I went to get her for lunch, and she was asleep. I turned her light off, figuring she needed the nap."

"Oh." Her body seemed to deflate. "Sorry."

"Sugar, I would *never* hurt her. Or you."

"I know that." She flapped her hand as if it was silly of me to suggest otherwise.

"Do you?"

"Of course I know that!" Her voice raised an octave. She began to pace, her tennis shoes barely making a sound on the hardwood. After several passes, she stopped in front of me and locked eyes with mine. "Look, I'm sorry. Can we start over? Please?"

I considered her question for a moment. A part of me wanted to say yes. To erase all of the anger, the hurt. But a bigger part of me realized it would be impossible for us to completely start over. I decided on a compromise.

"Not completely, no. But maybe we can start this day over." I reached out to brush an errant strand of hair behind her ear, leaving my palm to rest on her cheek.

Her eyes drifted closed as she leaned into my touch. "I'd like that." Her voice was a breathless whisper.

Unable to trust myself, I pulled my hand away and took a step back. Her eyes snapped open, and she pinned me with her stare.

"I, uh… are you hungry? There's more lunch meat if you'd like a sandwich." I didn't wait for her response before turning back toward the counter and busying myself making her lunch.

"Aiden?" She sounded tentative, confused. I couldn't blame her. I was confusing the hell out of myself.

"Yeah?"

"I really am sorry."

"For what?" I glanced over my shoulder so I could see her when she answered me.

Her chin dropped to her chest, but then she seemed to fortify herself with a deep breath. When she looked back up, she spread her arms out wide and shrugged. "For everything."

11

SCARLETT

"Hey, baby." I gently shook Tillie's shoulder to try and wake her. "It's time to get up."

She mumbled incoherently and turned onto her side with her back to me.

"Baby, c'mon. You've slept the day away." I smoothed my hand over her hair and then stroked her back. One of my favorite things was to watch her sleep and imagine all those little girl dreams she was having. But it was dinnertime, and I needed her to wake up. It was already going to be hard to get her to go to bed with this long of a nap. No need to make it any harder.

After a few minutes, Tillie's eyes slowly opened, and she rubbed them with her fists. "Mommy?"

"Hi, baby. Did you have a good nap?" I mentally winced at the question because I knew better than to utter the word 'nap'.

"Mommy, I a big girl. I don't take naps." Based on the attitude, her *nap* hadn't been long enough, despite the hours she'd slept.

"You're right. You are a big girl."

I pulled her onto my lap and tickled her, reveling in her giggle. She squirmed to get out of my hold, but I wasn't having it. I continued with my tickling antics until there was a knock on the door. At the sound, Tillie stiffened in my arms and her giggling immediately ceased.

Without waiting for a response, Aiden walked through the door and stood next to the bed, smiling down at us. Gone was the anger, the hurt, from earlier, but I knew it was a temporary reprieve. The afternoon had been spent with a series of awkward attempts at conversation and tense silences.

"How are my two favorite girls?" He reached down to ruffle Tillie's hair before leaning over to kiss my forehead. I had no idea how to interpret his actions or how to respond. Apparently, my body was a step ahead of my brain and heart because it began to tingle and heat at the contact.

"We's good," Tillie responded. Her body had relaxed after she'd seen Aiden, her initial fear gone.

"Did you have a good sleep?"

He knows not to say 'nap'.

I glared at him, frustration and jealousy battling at the ease with which he asked the question and at the fact that he remembered when I hadn't.

"Uh-huh. I had a dream about Sully."

At that moment, it hit me that I hadn't seen Sully since arriving earlier that day. I tried to recall if I'd seen a food or water bowl but couldn't remember. Sadie had said Sully was still around, but, if that was true, where was he? I asked Aiden as much.

"He's with Doc today. I didn't want him to be underfoot when we got home so you'd have a chance to get settled."

"Well, go get him." My tone was clipped, angry, but that anger wasn't directed at him. Guilt swamped me because this was Sully's home as much as it was Aiden's, yet he'd been shuffled off for me.

"Yay! Sully's coming home." Tillie jumped up to stand on the bed, pumping her fist in the air. "Let's go get him, Aiden. Can we go get him?" More guilt crashed into me at Tillie's excitement.

"Okay, peanut. Go put your shoes on and we'll go." Tillie was off the bed and out of the room before Aiden finished speaking. His gaze followed her, and he chuckled. When he turned back to face me, his smile fell. "What's wrong?"

"You're good with her." I stood before turning away from him to bend and straighten the covers on the bed.

"Scarlett, stop." His fingers brushed my arm and I tensed. The slap of his palm hitting his side as he dropped his hand seemed to echo in the room.

When I didn't turn around, he stepped closer to me, and the heat from his body seeped into mine, warming me from the inside out. I straightened and allowed myself to take everything he had to give in that moment. Maybe it was selfish, but I couldn't help it. I knew there were things that we needed to talk about, things he didn't know. Couple that with all the past hurt and taking anything from him was an epically horrible idea. I took anyway.

His breath whispered across my skin as he leaned in and nuzzled my neck. Shivers danced down my spine and settled between my legs.

"You always were so responsive to me." He growled in my ear.

He sucked the sensitive lobe between his lips and nibbled. I rocked back into him, grinding my ass against his now hard cock. My breathing had become choppy, and my head spun. As a moan escaped me, Tillie shouted for us, and it was as if someone poured a bucket of ice water over our heads. Aiden stiffened before stepping away from me. I turned around to face him. His stare was full of lust and promise. I didn't know whether to be scared or excited at what that look could mean.

"I guess that's our cue." I chuckled nervously as I glanced away from him.

"This isn't over, sugar." His hand tucked under my chin and forced me to look at him. "Not by a longshot." With that, he dropped his hand and turned to walk out the door.

I blew out a trembling breath, taking in his words. It took me a few minutes, but I eventually felt my frayed nerves settle and was able to join them in the living room. Tillie was bouncing up and down as Aiden attempted to tie her shoes. He was laughing at her antics, and she was laughing at him. It reminded me of the time I'd missed. The little moments with Tillie that reminded me of how lucky I was to have her. The time away from Aiden. The time we should have been spending as a family.

I shook my head to clear the dreary thoughts and went to stand by the door. "I'm ready." I tried to inject levity into my tone, but judging by Aiden's expression, I'd done a shitty job.

He cocked his head, and his brow furrowed. He must have decided that this wasn't the time or place to analyze my mood. The confused look left his face, and he bent to swing Tillie up into his arms, tossing her over his shoulder like a flour sack. The fact that she let him do that spoke volumes.

"Operation bring Sully home begins now." Aiden stepped toward the door, and I shuffled to the side to clear his way.

He kept a hand on Tillie's legs to hold her in place and opened the door with his free hand. I followed them out of the house, pulling the door shut behind me.

The ride to Doc's house was a short one, and when we pulled into his driveway, the door flew open and Sully bounded down the steps and ran toward the vehicle. The back half of his body wagged back and forth so fast, it was easy to see why Aiden had always called Boxers 'wiggle butts'.

"Mommy, Sully's happy to see us!" Tillie giggled in the backseat, and soon Aiden and I joined her.

"He sure is." I unbuckled my seatbelt and gripped the door handle before Aiden's voice stopped me.

"Wait for me to come around. He's a good dog, but he's hyper right now and I don't want him jumping on you and hurting you."

Aiden was out of the car and opened my door before getting Tillie out of her car seat. Tillie immediately fell to the ground to play with Sully, and he calmed down. It was like he knew he needed to be careful because she was a child.

I knelt next to her, and Sully tentatively stepped closer to me. I held out my hand for him to sniff, and after he did, his nub started wagging and he licked my face. He remembered me. Emotion clogged my throat, making it hard to breathe. Sully crawled into my lap, and I threw my arms around him and sobbed.

"Mommy, what's wrong?" Tillie stood up and placed a hand on my back. My sobs grew louder at the contact. "Aiden, something's wong wif mommy."

Aiden sat on the ground behind me and pulled me and Sully into his lap, wrapping us both in his strong arms. "Shhh, sugar, it's okay."

"It… it's not… o… okay," I wailed.

Aiden didn't say anything else, just rocked me back and forth and held me. I was dimly aware of another voice and Tillie walking away, but I couldn't control the gut-wrenching sadness. After what felt like a lifetime, the crying subsided and I was able to suck air into my lungs.

"I'm sorry." I scrubbed a hand over my face, wiping away the evidence of my breakdown.

"Why are you sorry?"

"Because I lost it."

As I became more aware of my surroundings, two things became clear. Tillie wasn't anywhere I could see her, and I was being poked in the ass by something. I looked over my shoulder at Aiden, my eyes narrowed in suspicion.

"Don't look at me like that." He lifted me slightly and pushed me off his lap. "I can't help it."

"Where's Tillie?" I chose to ignore the fact that me having a meltdown gave him a hard-on.

"Inside with Doc." He nodded toward the house. "Emersyn is off today, so I imagine she's sneaking her cookies."

"Who's Emersyn?"

"Doc's wife. She's also a nurse, which is great because we always seem to have someone that needs medical care." He chuckled and shook his head. Then he stood and stuck his hand out to help me up. "C'mon. Let's go get her and go home."

I stared at his hand a moment before taking it and allowing him to pull me to my feet. I brushed grass off my ass and shoved my hair behind my ears. My feet didn't move as I watched him walk toward the porch. When he noticed I wasn't following, he looked back and caught me smoothing my shirt.

"You look great. Stop worrying." He smiled and stood there, waiting for me.

Satisfied that I was as good as I was going to get, I jogged to him and we both went inside. Once the screen door shut behind us, Tillie came running and slid to a stop on the hardwood floor.

"Where's Sully?" She may seem so grown up sometimes, but she was all four-year-old little girl.

"He's outside waiting for you, peanut. Why don't you put your shoes on and we can take him home?" Aiden bent to pick up her shoes that were sitting on a rug next to the door and handed them to her.

"You leaving us, sweetie?" A stunningly beautiful woman walked into the room wiping her hands on a dishtowel. She wore an apron and a perfect smile.

"We haf to take Sully home." Tillie spoke to the woman like she knew her well.

"Ah, okay." The woman stuck her hand out to me. "Hi. I'm Emersyn. You must be Scarlett. It's nice to meet you."

"Uh, yes, I'm Scarlett." I shook her hand and smiled. Emersyn had kind eyes, and my daughter seemed to like her, which made me happy. "Thanks for looking out for her just now."

"No need to thank me. We love spending time with the kids. It's good practice." She winked at Tillie and then rubbed a circle over her stomach.

"Em, I thought we weren't telling anyone?" A man walked up behind Emersyn and wrapped his arms around her waist. He kissed her cheek from behind.

"Wait a minute. Are you…?" Aiden nodded toward the couple's joined hands and they both nodded. "Holy shit! Why didn't you say anything?"

"You said the bad word." Tillie stepped in front of Aiden and held out a hand. "That's a dollar for the jar."

"Well, sh… crap." Aiden pulled his wallet out of his back pocket and handed a dollar to Tillie. "Hold on to that until we get home, peanut." When his penance was complete, he looked back at them. "So?"

"There's been a lot going on, and we wanted to be sure." The man stepped away from Emersyn and came to stand in front of me. "I'm Maddoc. Everyone calls me Doc though."

"Not me. And Auntie Sadie and Auntie Brie don't call you Doc." Tillie stepped between Doc and me and tugged on his shirt.

He chuckled and bent to scoop her into his arms. Tillie giggled and squealed when he spun her around in circles. "You're right, munchkin. There are some people that call me Maddoc."

When he set her down on her feet he returned his attention back to me. "Call me whatever you want. Makes no difference to me."

"Well, it's nice to meet you Maddoc." I shook his hand and noticed that his grip was firm. He didn't treat me like I was broken, and for that, I was grateful. "And congrats."

"Thanks. We're excited." Maddoc returned to his place by his wife and wrapped an arm around her waist, pulling her to him. "Seven months and we'll join the parenthood ranks." He kissed her on the cheek again, and I had to look away.

My eyes landed on Aiden's face, and while he was grinning, it didn't reach his eyes. He stared at them for a moment longer before he looked down at Tillie and then at me. His grin slipped away and his head fell. He wrung his hands and drew in a deep breath.

"We, uh, should get going." He picked Tillie up and it seemed he held her a little tighter.

"Yay! I wanna pway wif Sully." Tillie didn't notice the extra pressure of his hug, but I did.

"I'm happy for you guys. We should all get together and celebrate." Aiden turned toward the door, but before he opened it and stepped outside, he glanced over his shoulder. "Just wait, Doc. There's no better feeling in the world than being a father." He walked out and left me standing there, staring at his back.

I froze, unable to make my feet follow. A muscled arm came around my shoulders.

"He'll be fine. Trust me." Maddoc's voice was smooth, like a good whiskey.

"He hates me," I mumbled.

"Oh, honey, he doesn't hate you. He may hate that he missed out on time with Tillie, but never you." He stepped in front of me and forced my head up to look into his eyes. "He looked for you, ya know? The day you left, a piece of him left with you. He wasn't the same after that. But one thing never changed. He loved you. Hell, he still does. He never gave up on you, so don't give up on him."

"I didn't know. I thought…"

"Stop. It doesn't matter what you didn't know then. What matters is what you do now with what you know."

I nodded and said my goodbyes before I walked out the door and joined Aiden, Tillie, and Sully in the vehicle.

"What was that all about?" Aiden asked as I closed the door.

"Nothing."

Aiden put the car in gear and drove us back to his place. Conversation between him and Tillie flowed, but I remained silent.

He looked for me. He never gave up. The big question was, now that I knew, what was I going to do about it?

12

AIDEN

"Why didn't you tell me you looked for me?"

When we'd gotten home, Tillie had gone straight to her room to play, and Sully had followed, leaving Scarlett and me alone in the living room. She'd been quiet up until then and I'd started to worry, but when she'd asked that question, my worry became more about how to answer than about her silence.

"Would it have changed anything?"

"I don't know." Scarlett looked at me with confusion scrunching her face and shrugged. "Maybe."

"Scarlett, you know as well as I do that it wouldn't have changed a damn thing." She looked away from me and stared at the wall, but I didn't let that deter me. "You left. I'm sure you had your reasons, but it hurt."

"I thought I was doing the right thing." When she faced me again, there was a glint of determination in her eyes, a spark that hadn't been there since seeing her that first day in the hospital. "I was young, pregnant and barely knew you and—"

"You knew me enough to fuck me. To sleep in my bed

every night." I spat the words out like they were poison. "You knew me enough to have my baby."

"That's not fair." She shot up off the couch and began to pace. "Yes, I slept with you. Yes, I got pregnant. Yes, I had your baby. But I had to leave."

"Why? What was so goddamn important that you had to walk away and keep my child from me for four years?"

She whirled around, and her face was red with rage. "I was protecting you!"

"You expect me to believe that? You came to the BRB for protection. We were protecting you!"

"You don't understand." Her shoulders slumped and breath rushed past her parted lips.

I stood and walked toward her, placing my hands on her shoulders. "Then make me understand."

Scarlett pulled out of my grasp and began to pace again. After several passes across the room, she squared her shoulders and stopped to face me.

"When I was here before, I told you I had a stalker."

"I remember. What does that have to do with why you left?"

"Everything." She sat on the couch and tipped her head to the empty space next to her. "Sit, please. I can't talk to you when you're standing there staring at me."

I sat, but not next to her. I sat on the coffee table in front of her. She'd just have to get used to me looking at her because I didn't plan on stopping. Besides, I needed to see her face as she told me her story so I could tell what was real and what was fake. I didn't yet trust her not to lie, but what her words couldn't tell me, her eyes could.

"I did have a stalker when I showed up here. He was my ex. Problem was, he couldn't accept that."

Truth.

"Go on."

"We'd dated while I was in college. He was great at first. An army brat like me." She rubbed her hands up and down her thighs, and my eyes tracked the movement. "My dad was, *is*, stationed overseas. When I started school, it was the first time I'd had any freedom. My parents were always overprotective, like they were determined to never let any of the evil in the world touch me."

I could understand why. The things I'd seen as a Navy Seal were burned into my memory, and I wouldn't want any of it to ever touch Tillie.

"Okay, so you did what most college kids do."

"It was more than that though. Justin was ev—" She slapped a hand over her mouth when she realized what she'd just revealed.

"Sugar, I already knew his name."

"How?" She dropped her hand, and her brows furrowed.

"I have my ways." I wasn't about to tell her that Sadie had told me. I wanted her to feel comfortable around my friends, not betrayed.

"Anyway, he started to get possessive, controlling." She looked past me, staring at something invisible in the room. "I'd talked to my parents about it, and my dad was worried. I blew it off like I always did. Then one day, Justin followed me to the library where I was with a study group. He flipped out. The group was made up of me and another girl, but there were also three guys and Justin didn't like that. He accused me of cheating on him and dragged me back to the apartment where he proceeded to rage at me for hours. When he was done, he went to bed like nothing was wrong."

"Did he hit you?"

She shook her head. "Not that night. I waited until he was asleep and packed a bag and walked out. I left him a note, breaking things off with him and told him a friend would pick up the rest of my stuff."

So far, everything was the truth, which only served to fuel my anger. I wanted to track the bastard down and fuck his world up the way he had hers.

"He left me alone for a while. I stayed in school and was close to graduating when weird things began to happen."

"What kind of weird things?"

"Letters taped to my door, never any signature. Flowers in my car when I'd get out of class. It wasn't anything scary, but at the same time, it was." She shrugged. "I knew it was him but I ignored it at first. Then one night, after work, he was waiting outside for me."

My entire body tensed, not wanting to hear what she had to say, but needing to hear it.

"He begged and pleaded to get back together. I told him 'no' and he lost it." She fixed her stare on me, and my heart dropped. "That was the night I showed up here."

She'd shown up on my doorstep scared out of her mind. She'd said she had a stalker but that she didn't know who it was. She'd lied that night. But she wasn't lying now.

"All of that sucks, and I'm sorry it happened." I drew in a deep breath. "But that still doesn't explain why you left."

She took a deep breath before answering. "I left because he found me."

Lie.

"Wanna try that again, sugar?"

"What? Why?"

"Because up until then, you were being honest. But there's more to the story. You didn't leave because he found you. At least, that's not the only reason. You were pregnant and you just went back to a guy who scared you? I'm not buying it."

Scarlett stood and walked to the fireplace. I wasn't happy that I couldn't see her eyes, but I didn't budge. She was going to talk, whether it be now or later. I would get the truth.

"Why are you doing this?" Her voice was barely above a whisper.

"Doing what? Making you face the truth?"

"Yes."

"Because I have to know why I missed out on so much. I just… have to."

She turned toward me, silently pleading for me to let her stop. I met her stare and didn't waver.

"Fine," she huffed. "When he found me, it wasn't long after I got here."

"How long?" I demanded.

"Two weeks." She dropped her head and wrung her hands.

"Two fucking weeks?! You were here for months and never said anything."

"Don't you think I know that? Aiden, you have to understand." She took a few tentative steps toward me. "He never actually hurt me. Scared me sometimes, yes. But he was never violent. And he was my first love."

"*I* loved you. You were *my* first love."

She winced at my words but nothing in me wanted to call them back. She needed to understand how much she meant to me. How much her leaving had hurt.

"I loved you too. I loved you both. But when I found out I was pregnant? That scared me more than anything. I'd been here for months, and this place? Aiden, there was always something going on with a client. Some dangerous situation that you were in. What if something had happened to you? Raising a baby with Justin seemed like the better option."

"He stalked you!"

"I know! I didn't say I made the right decision. But it's the one I made, and I can't change that."

"Mommy?"

Both of us whirled around at the sound of our daughter's

voice. She was rubbing her eye with a tiny fist and holding a teddy bear in the other hand. Sully sat next to her, tongue hanging out the side of his mouth.

"Hey, baby." Scarlett rushed to Tillie's side and crouched down in front of her. "What's wrong?"

"You guys is fighting." Tillie's bottom lip poked out. "I don't like it when people fight."

"Oh, baby. We're not fighting." Scarlett threw a look over her shoulder, practically daring me to contradict her. "We were just talking. Everything's fine. I promise." She pulled Tillie in for a hug, and Tillie's arms came around her neck.

Scarlett rose while holding Tillie and turned to face me, questions dancing in her eyes.

"Go." I nodded toward Tillie's room. "We'll finish this later."

Scarlett gave a tight nod, turned and walked out of the room.

I stood rooted to the same spot for long moments, listening to the sounds of them moving around in the bedroom. Sully had followed them, and every few seconds his bark would reach my ears. Each time it did, Tillie's giggle followed.

I rubbed a hand over my chest. Anger warred with sadness and knotted in my gut. Scarlett was right. She couldn't change the choice she'd made. But maybe, just maybe, I could make her see that I was still the choice she *should* have made. That I was the man that she should always choose. Because despite what she had done, I still loved her. And nothing was going to change that.

Nothing ever could.

13

SCARLETT

"You look pwetty, mommy."

I tied Tillie's shoes before zipping up her coat. She was spending the day with Aiden, Micah, and the twins while I went shopping with Sadie and Brie. Nell and Emersyn wanted to come, but they had to work.

"Thank you, baby." I kissed my daughter's cheek and stood. "You are the prettiest little girl in the whole wide world."

"I'll second that."

I whirled around at the sound of Aiden's voice, and my mouth watered. He was dressed in worn dark wash jeans and a grey Henley. His muscles bunched under the long-sleeved tee that fit him to perfection.

"Take a picture, it'll last longer." He shoved his hands in his pockets and rocked back on his heels.

"Funny." His smart-ass comment snapped me out of the trance his body had put me in.

I walked past him to get my jacket from the closet, careful not to touch him. I heard him chuckle, and that sent frustration coursing through me. Aiden Winters was infuriating. He was the only man that could have me thinking about wild sex one minute and wanting to strangle him the next.

"What's wrong, sugar?" He was behind me, his hands braced on the door frame of the closet, boxing me in and leaning close to my ear. "You seem… agitated."

I was agitated all right. I just didn't know if it was from the lust or the frustration. Who was I kidding? It was both, which only fueled the fire in my veins. In more ways than one.

The sound of footsteps on the porch saved me from responding. There was a sharp knock on the door before it opened, and Micah stepped over the threshold. He looked at Aiden and me, raised his eyebrows and then shook his head.

"What?" Aiden snapped.

"Nothing." Micah focused his attention on Tillie. "You ready to go, munchkin? Isaiah and Izzy are excited to spend the day with you."

"Yeah." Tillie raced to Micah and let him pick her up. He tickled her in the ribs, and her innocent little girl giggles warmed my heart. He was so good with her.

Almost as good as her father is.

I shook the thought from my head and ducked under Aiden's arm to say goodbye to Tillie. Aiden dropped his chin but didn't move.

"I'll wait in the car for you." Micah carried Tillie outside, and I stood at the door watching him walk away with my reason for living.

When they were both in the car, I started to turn around, but Aiden was next to me, frowning.

"Are we going to tip-toe around this forever?"

"I don't know what you're talking about." I tried to step away, but he gripped my forearm.

"You know damn well what I'm talking about. Why are you fighting this?"

"Aiden, not now. Go spend the day with your friend and your daughter."

"If not now, then when? There's always something that stops us from talking." He dropped his hands to his sides, allowing me to put some space between us. "You can't really think that you can tell me you love me and that's the end of it."

"Loved, Aiden. Past tense."

"Bullshit."

"Please, don't do this." A headache started to form at my temple, and I rubbed at it, hoping to ease the pain.

A car horn honked, and his head fell back.

"Okay. You win." With that, he walked out the door and didn't look back.

When he was gone, I sat on the couch and wondered what was holding me back. I wanted to talk to Aiden, tell him about the last four years. I wanted to tell him everything about Tillie… what he hadn't already figured out on his own. And I also wanted to tell him that I needed time. That I needed to figure out who I was when I wasn't being hunted. That I wanted time to be a mother to Tillie without fear being the primary emotion.

I wanted to tell him that my love for him wasn't past tense. And I wanted him to tell me that he wanted me, not because he felt some misguided sense of duty because we had Tillie, but because he loved me too.

∼

"I pay my own way."

Sadie had pulled out her credit card, again, to pay for the clothes I'd picked out. While I appreciated the gesture, I had my own money, and a lot of it, despite what people thought or the way I'd lived the last four years.

"We know you can, but you shouldn't. Not now." Brie put her hand on my shoulder and squeezed it. "Not when we don't know if he's still out there."

"He is." I narrowed my eyes and took a deep breath. "But I won't let him control any more of my life."

"Of course not. That's not what we're saying." Sadie signed the receipt because clearly I hadn't been fast enough to stop her from paying. "But think about Tillie. Do you really want to take any chances until we know for sure that he's going to leave you alone?"

"Low blow." I grabbed the bag off the counter and walked toward the door, knowing they'd follow me.

"I'm sorry, Scarlett. That wasn't my intention." Sadie looked genuinely upset that she may have hurt me.

"It's fine." As I got in the back seat of the Jeep, my thoughts wandered, but not for long.

"So, if you don't want to talk about *him*, then let's talk about Aiden." Brie turned around in the passenger seat to face me.

"Brie! We said we weren't going to talk about that," Sadie admonished.

"There's nothing to talk about. He's helping out with Tillie while I figure out my next move."

"Oh, please. I've seen the way you two look at each other. There's way more there than him spending time with his daughter." Apparently, Sadie wasn't completely sold on 'not talking about it'.

"Look, I'm not going to deny that there's an… attraction. But I can't go there right now."

"Why not?" Sadie pulled into the lot at the next store on our trip. She put the vehicle in park and twisted in her seat. "You love him. He loves you. You have a daughter together. Seems to me, that's a little more than basic attraction."

I ducked my head at her words. Was she right? Did he love me?

No. Not going there.

"I wouldn't be so sure." I reached for the door handle and Brie engaged the locks so I couldn't get out. Damn child lock.

"We're not done." Brie smiled to soften the harshly spoken statement. "What makes you think that?"

"Aiden hates me. Sure, he wants to sleep with me." I waved my hand in a dismissive gesture. "But I left him, kept his daughter from him. There's no way that he still has real feelings for me."

"Fuck, you really believe that, don't you?"

"Do you blame her?" Sadie looked toward Brie. "I mean, we know the truth, but I'm sure there's plenty we don't know. Like why she's fighting this so hard."

"You two are ridiculous, you know that, right?" I chuckled because it was hard to be angry at their meddling. They meant well.

"Yes, we do. Thank you." Brie gave a cheeky grin.

"Okay, here's the deal." I took a deep breath and explained things the best I could. "It feels like there's more there between us. At least there was four years ago. When I'm around him, I feel, I don't know. Complete? But that scares the shit out of me. There's so much he doesn't know, and I maintain the fact that I still don't know him that well."

"But you want to get to know him?" Sadie's eyes held a spark of determination.

"Well, yeah, I guess. But more than that, I want him to get to know me. I don't want him to be with me because he feels he has to be."

"Oh, honey, you have nothing to worry about on that front." Brie pulled out her cell phone and scrolled through some pictures until she found what she was looking for. She turned the screen to me and asked, "What do you see here?"

I looked at the image, unsure why she was showing it to me. "It looks like a wedding photo of you two with your husbands."

She slid her finger across the screen and displayed a dozen other photos of what appeared to be their double wedding. When she was done, she dropped her cell into her lap.

"Did you notice anything odd about those pics?"

"Um, no?" I had no idea what she was trying to prove.

"Did you see Aiden in any of them?" Her eyebrows rose and she pinned me with her stare.

I thought back to the images. "No."

"And do you know why he's not in any of the pictures?"

"No."

"It was the craziest thing." Brie looked to her friend and Sadie gave a tight nod. "Ya see, Aiden was the best man at our wedding. Griffin is his best friend, and he and Micah are like brothers to Aiden. But after the ceremony, he got a text. One simple text and he was gone. Didn't come back at all that night. Not for pictures, not to celebrate with his *family*. Not for anything."

"Okay." I dragged the word out, still not sure what her point was. "I'm sorry he left, but that doesn't mean—"

"The text was from you." Sadie took control of the conversation. "He left that night." She held up her hand when I opened my mouth to speak. "And that's okay. We understood. But when he came back the next morning, it was like a switch had been flipped."

"Oh my god." The words whooshed out of me as it all came flooding back. "I remember that night. I'd texted him because I thought Justin had given up. I wanted to meet with him. Tell him about Tillie. But when I pulled into the bar parking lot, Justin's car was there. I sped out of the lot so fast and didn't look back."

"Wait a second." Brie had a shell-shocked look at my revelation. "Are you saying that Aiden's seen Justin before? That he was here and was the reason you didn't show that night?"

"He wouldn't have known it was him, but yeah. I, um… I'd been running for a while. Tillie had been overseas with my parents. I was going to tell Aiden everything and see if the BRB would take me on as a client again so I could bring her back to the states. I needed her back with me."

Tears began to gather at the corners of my eyes, and I sniffled. Sadie handed me a tissue and gave me a sympathetic smile.

"Scarlett, he'd have protected you both. But not as a client. He'd have protected you because Tillie's family. By extension, you're family. All of that aside, he'd have protected you because he loves you."

"But what if you're wrong? That was a long time ago and I hurt him. Badly."

"Listen to me," Brie spoke up. "I have an idea. If you're so concerned that he's doing what he's doing out of some archaic notion that he has to, then why don't you move out?"

"I don't understand. What would that prove? And weren't you both just telling me earlier that I shouldn't be foolish while Justin is still out there?"

"Well, yes, but we could kill two birds with one stone." Brie spoke with excitement.

"Brie, no." Sadie's tone held a hint of warning and until she spoke again, I had no idea why. "Scarlett and Tillie can't be used as bait."

"It's perfect." The thrill in Brie's voice didn't diminish. "If she moves into a place of her own, then she will see that Aiden's not going anywhere. That he's in this for the long haul and not because he has to be. They can date, like normal people."

"I get that part and think it's a great idea," Sadie relented. "But that would put her and Tillie at risk."

"No, it wouldn't. We'd set up the best security system, and she'd have around the clock protection detail. The guys are good. If Justin shows up, he'll never know anyone is watching."

"That's a horri—"

"I love it." Sadie carefully masked her annoyance with my agreement. "I want this whole thing to be over. I'm tired of running."

"Scarlett, this is dangerous." Sadie was worried but I wasn't. Not really. I knew that, even if he didn't love me, Aiden would protect me. And Tillie.

"I can handle dangerous. I've been doing it for the last four years." I was warming up to the idea but for a far more important reason that what they had suggested. "Besides, I need this. I need to give Tillie a home and put down some roots. And I need to do it alone. She needs to see her mother being strong and not running or relying on others to provide for us."

"Sounds like a plan to me." Brie picked her cell up from her lap and tapped the screen to bring it to life. "I say we skip the rest of the shopping trip and go look at apartments."

"Don't you think Aiden should be a part of that?" Sadie looked at me expectantly.

"Well, I don't have to make any decisions today." I shrugged. "But I think it'd be fun. Let's do it."

"I just want it on record that I protested this." Sadie started the vehicle and pulled out of the parking lot.

"Duly noted," Brie said. "Now, there's an apartment for rent about twenty minutes from here." She continued to scroll through her phone looking at what I presumed were rental properties. Brie was nothing if not hard-headed and determined. "Oh, oh, look at this!" She turned the phone for me to see. "That's such a cute little house. It'd be perfect for you and Tillie."

"Wow. Tillie and I have never lived in a house. We've always had apartments."

"You could have a house if you stayed with Aiden." Sadie was following the directions that Brie gave her, but she wasn't happy about it.

"I could. But then I'd always wonder, ya know?" The more and more I thought about Tillie and me living on our own, the more I warmed up to the idea.

And if it turned out that I was right and Aiden wasn't stepping up out of love then there wouldn't be any awkwardness. We'd already have a home, and Aiden would still be close enough to spend time with his daughter.

14

AIDEN

"What do you mean, you're moving out?"

Panic gripped me in a way it never had before. I'd just gotten her back and now she was walking out again. Only this time, I knew exactly how much I was losing.

"Aiden, the girls and I—"

"The girls? What do they have to do with this?" I picked up my phone and tapped a green icon.

"What are you doing?"

"Calling Micah and Griffin. They need to get their wives under control."

I scrolled through my recent calls list until Griffin's name appeared. Just when I was about to hit 'call', Scarlett snatched the phone from my hand.

"You will do no such thing. They have the kids at the park and you're not ruining Tillie's fun because of this. Besides, this wasn't Sadie and Brie's decision. It was mine." She folded her arms over her chest, her cleavage heaving in anger. "I can't stay here forever, Aiden. Tillie and I need to have a home, not just a temporary place to rest our heads."

"You have a home. Here, with me." Fury infused my words. "You will not leave me again!"

"You don't get to tell me what I can and can't do. You're not my father!"

"You're right, I'm not. But I'm Tillie's, and I won't let you take her from me." I took a few steps to stand directly in front of her and noticed that her face had paled. That didn't stop me. "You already stole years from me. I won't let you take any more."

Scarlett backed up a few steps and stared at me. Color began to infuse her cheeks again, and I could see her temper manifesting in her body language.

"I did what I had to do. What I thought was right. I can't change it, and I don't expect you to forget, but I do suggest you find a way to forgive."

The conversation had gotten out of control quickly. When she'd gotten home from shopping the other day, she'd been happy. At the time, I'd been so grateful that she was smiling and not thinking about the shit that had landed her in the hospital, I hadn't questioned why. I wished that I had.

"You do realize that Justin is still out there. We haven't been able to track him down." There, that should scare some sense into her.

"I'm well aware of the threat, asshole." She uncrossed her arms and dropped them to her sides. "But it's nothing I haven't faced before. And that was when I didn't have the BRB as backup."

While I was glad she felt safe enough with the Broken Rebel Brotherhood as her protection, it also infuriated me. I wanted her to feel safe with *me*.

She came to you, not the Brotherhood.

"Look, will you at least come check the house out? I want you to be a part of this decision, if for no other reason than it's where your daughter will be living. I'm not trying to cut you out of her life, Aiden." Her eyes were luminous pools of melted sapphire and in that moment, I couldn't refuse her.

I was still pissed as hell, but she was stubborn and wouldn't let up. That much I knew. Besides, it was better this way. At least she wouldn't be taking off in the middle of the night. I hoped.

"Fine." I scooped my bike key off the table and turned toward the door.

"Where are you going?" Her footsteps echoed off the hardwood floor as she walked toward me, uncertainty in her voice.

"We're going to look at this house." I glanced over my shoulder just in time to see her smile widen.

"Thank you." She jumped up and threw her arms around my neck.

I breathed in her scent. A hint of vanilla with honey. I wrapped my arms around her and held on tight. She turned her face and kissed me on the cheek. Her arms loosened, and she slid down my body, the contact going straight to my cock. When her feet hit the floor, we locked eyes and her breath hitched.

"Do you have any idea what you do to me?" My voice was gravelly, sexually charged.

She glanced down between our bodies and took in the bulge straining at my zipper. When she looked back up, she caught her bottom lip between her teeth.

"Sugar, you're playing with fire." I traced her cheekbone with my thumb before running it over her parted lips.

She snaked her tongue out and curled it around my thumb, pulling it into her mouth with intoxicating suction. When she wrapped her lips around it and slid them to the tip, I couldn't help but envision another time her mouth was wrapped around something thick.

"Scarlett…"

"Hmm?"

"If you keep that up, we're not going anywhere."

She hummed, sending shockwaves through me. She released my thumb and dropped to her knees, unbuckling my belt as she went. As much as I wanted what she was offering, I wanted something else more. I leaned down and lifted her up and against the wall. Her legs went around me, and she locked her ankles at the small of my back.

Angling my head, I fused my lips with hers, sweeping my tongue past the seam. With my body holding her up, I braced myself with my hands against the wall above her head. Her hands explored my chest through my shirt, and I needed more. I needed skin. I slid my hands under her ass and spun her around and set her on her feet.

I tore my shirt off over my head and tossed it on the floor. She stood rooted to her spot and tracked my every movement. I tugged my zipper down and lowered my jeans and boxer briefs. My cock sprang free and her eyes immediately zeroed in on it, widening a bit.

"Look at me," I demanded.

She slowly raised her head, and her eyes met mine. I thought she was going to put a stop to what we were about to do but she surprised me. With her gaze never wavering, she took three steps back and stripped off her clothes, one article at a time. When we were both naked, I closed the distance between us and lifted her back up and turned, bracing her on the wall.

Her wet heat spurred me on. I bent my head and sucked a pebbled nipple into my mouth. Her head thumped back against the wall, and her breathy moans filled the air.

"Oh, God." She trembled in my arms.

"Not God, honey. Just Aiden." I switched to the other nipple and traced lazy circles with my tongue.

"Ahh, fuck. I need... Aiden, please..."

"Please what, sugar?" I carried her away from the wall toward the couch, my hands locked under her ass, my thumbs tantalizing that tight hole as I walked.

She licked her lips and her lids slid closed. "It's, uh, been a while," she whispered.

Her words stopped me in my tracks. "How long?"

"Long enough." Her eyes opened, and her face flushed.

"How. Long?"

"Four years and nine months. Roughly." She'd turned her head away from me, embarrassed.

How was that possible? She left me for her fucking ex. Not wanting those thoughts to ruin this, I pushed them to the back of my mind and focused on the woman in my arms. Now that I knew just how long of a dry spell she'd had, I needed to slow things down. I changed my course and carried her into the bedroom, kicking the door closed behind me.

I deposited her on the bed and leaned over her.

"Are you sure about this?" I wanted this, more than I wanted my next breath, but did she?

Rather than answer, she nodded and pulled my head down to fuse our mouths. I deepened the kiss and crawled up the bed to align our bodies. While we kissed, I reached down and glided a finger over her clit. She was wet and ready for me. I circled the sensitive knot several times before sliding that finger into her pussy. Her walls clamped down, and her body bucked. I added a second digit and finger fucked her until she was right on the edge.

When I thought she was about to break, I pulled my fingers out and broke off the kiss. I stared her in the eyes while I lined my cock up and thrust into her. Her eyes rolled, and her body arched to meet mine. Heat surrounded me, making control almost obsolete. It might not have been as long for me, but no one had ever made me feel the way Scarlett did.

She locked her legs around my waist and met me thrust for thrust. I'd wanted to go slow, but each time I tried to slow things down, she ran her nails down my back, spurring me on. One last thrust and her body stiffened as her walls spasmed around my cock. That was all it took for me to fall into oblivion with her.

I collapsed on top of her, all strength gone. Her arms and legs fell to the bed and her body relaxed. We were both sweaty and the smell of sex wafted around us. My dick slid out of her, and the sticky wetness had me tensing.

"Fuck." I shoved myself off of her and sat on the edge of the bed. I braced my elbows on my knees and hung my head.

Scarlett sat up behind me and wrapped her arms around my shoulders. "What's wrong?"

"I forgot to use a rubber." I shook my head. "Shit. I'm sorry."

"Oh." She flopped back onto the bed, taking her body heat with her. "Well, maybe we'll get lucky."

She didn't sound convinced. I'd fucked up and I knew it.

"Just promise me something?" I turned and drew a knee up onto the bed.

"What?" She eyed me skeptically.

"If you get pregnant, you won't leave again. Promise me you won't leave again."

"Aiden, I can't—"

"Promise me, Scarlett," I snapped.

She blew out a breath and took another deep one. "I promise I won't keep it from you if I get pregnant."

That wasn't exactly what I'd asked, but it would have to be good enough. I stood and walked to the bathroom to clean up. I brought a warm washcloth back to her and wiped away the evidence of our lack of self-control.

"Come on. Let's get dressed."

"Aiden, are you angry?" She sat up on her knees and grabbed my hand to stop me from walking away again.

"No. Yes." I huffed out a breath. "I don't know. Maybe." I broke free of her hold and increased my distance from her. "Let's go look at that house."

15

SCARLETT

"What about Sully, mommy?"

Tillie and I were moving into the new house today, and she was struggling with leaving the now-familiar surroundings of Aiden's place. He had given his approval of the small two-bedroom house, provided the landlord approved the security updates he and the guys wanted to install. The day the landlord had given the 'okay', I'd signed the lease and paid first months rent and security deposit… in cash. That was a week ago.

"You can visit Sully any time you want, and he can also come to the house to play with you." I brushed the hair back from her forehead.

Aiden, with help from Micah and Griffin, had spent the last few days installing what he said was a top of the line security system and making sure it worked the way he wanted. My cute little house now had security cameras in every room, as well as monitors so I could keep an eye on everything going on. Motion sensor lights had been installed at the front and back of the house that lit up the yard like fireworks on the fourth of July. It was a bit much if you asked me, but it made Aiden feel better and complain less about us moving.

"You ready to go?" Aiden stood in the doorway of Tillie's room with his arms crossed over his chest. He was smiling, but I knew it was more for Tillie's benefit than mine.

"Just about," I said to him before returning my attention to Tillie. "Baby, go get your shoes on so we can go. We'll be out in a minute."

Tillie ran out of the room so fast I was worried she'd trip over her own two feet, but she didn't. Aiden simply stood there, shaking his head and chuckling at her.

"I wish I had half of her energy." His face sobered, and he stared at me. "Are you sure about this, sugar? I'd feel better if you both stayed here."

"It's a little late to change my mind. I put down a large chunk of cash for that house and all of the furniture has been delivered." I stood and closed the distance between us. "Besides, I want this."

"I'm still not real clear about how you were able to afford everything." He rubbed the side of his nose, a move I quickly determined meant he was uncomfortable.

"I told you, I have a pretty good size nest egg from my grandparents, and I worked a lot of jobs for cash after I left."

"I still can't get over the fact that you're rich. Fuck, that security system alone was over ten grand." He pushed off the doorframe and stood straight, towering over me.

"You're kinda making my point. You know that, right?" I tilted my head and watched as his jaw hardened and his eyes narrowed. "We don't really know each other."

"We know enough." He reached out to grab my hand, but I pulled away. Hurt flashed in his eyes, and I hated that I'd put it there. He threaded a hand through his hair, disheveling it in the process.

"Aiden, please. Don't do this. If not for me, then for your daughter. I don't want her to see us fighting."

"We're not fighting. We're disagreeing. There's a difference." He turned away from me and walked to the living room where Tillie waited on the couch. "Ready, peanut?" He asked as he ruffled her hair.

"Uh-huh." She hopped off the couch and went to the door, throwing it open. "I'm wedy."

There wasn't anything to load into the car because we hadn't had anything when I'd ended up in the hospital. What little Tillie had accumulated since then would be staying at Aiden's place, so it was as much a home to her as the little rented house. We'd purchased all brand new belongings and wardrobes, and it all waited at the new place for us. I had stuff in storage but decided that this was a fresh start and I didn't need it. It'd be donated to a local charity. Sadie and Brie were handling the details so that my name wasn't attached to it. Less chance of being tracked that way.

The drive to the yellow sided two-story was tense. Tillie babbled about anything and everything, and Aiden and I gave an appropriate amount of head nods and responses to keep her satisfied that we were paying attention. Neither of us were.

When Aiden pulled into the driveway, I smiled at the white fence that surrounded the yard and the perfectly manicured lawn and landscaping. The flowers were beautiful, and they put me in a good mood. It was one of the things I loved about it. And I'd spent an inordinately large amount of money on a security system that didn't detract from the aesthetic of the house. I couldn't see any of it if I wasn't looking hard enough.

"Look, Scarlett." I whirled around when Aiden spoke. "I, uh, know I haven't exactly acted like it, but I just want you to be happy."

"I know." I placed my hand over his on the center console and smiled. "This makes me happy, Aiden. More than you could possibly understand."

"I can see that. But…"

"But what?" He wasn't normally shy but at that moment, he reminded me of a schoolboy with no clue how to talk to a girl.

"I want to know. There's still so much you haven't told me." He placed a finger over my lips when they parted. "I know, that's kind of the whole point. But we still have a lot to talk about. And I'm not just talking our favorite movies or food."

I took a deep breath and blew it out. "Why don't you come over tomorrow and we'll talk?"

"Really?" His eyes widened in surprise.

"Yeah. You're right. If I expect you to protect me and Tillie, you have to know everything. It's not a pretty story. But it's my story. Mine and Tillie's."

"Sounds like a plan. Does six work? That gives me time to do some work during the day."

"Perfect." I opened the door and stepped out before turning back around and leaning into the car. "And Aiden?"

"Huh?"

"Sweet Home Alabama and peanut butter ice cream." My smile grew. "Favorite movie and food."

I heard his chuckle as I shut the door.

∽

"I think that about covers it."

"Oh, is that all?" I slumped down on the brand new leather couch and looked around at my surroundings.

"Yep." Aiden sat beside me but not so close that we were touching. "Unless you want me to go over something again."

"God, no. I think I've had enough tech for one day." I hugged a pillow to my chest and curled my legs under me. "Are you sure this is all necessary? I mean, it seems like a little much."

"Maybe, but why take the chance? Isn't it better to be a little overprotected than not protected enough?" He looked toward the stairs and tipped his head towards them. "Besides, there's precious cargo in the house."

He was referring to Tillie, who was now sound asleep in her new room. We'd painted the room a sky blue color and everything else was unicorns. Tillie had said that she already had a princess room at Aiden's and wanted something different. And I wanted her to have whatever she wanted, so I'd given it to her.

With the help of Aiden and his friends, we'd transformed every room in the house to reflect what I thought of when I thought of a home. I couldn't be happier with the results. I hadn't thought I would like the place any more than I did at that first walkthrough, but I was completely in love with it now.

A long silence had elapsed, and suddenly, Aiden shifted to face me. "Promise me that if anything happens or even if you just feel like something is off, you'll call me."

"Aiden, I—"

"Promise me."

"I promise I'll call."

"I don't care what time it is, Scarlett."

"Okay."

My cell phone pinged from the barn wood coffee table. I picked it up and tapped the screen to bring up the full text. I grinned and typed out a quick response, then set it face down on my thigh.

"Who was that?" Suspicion laced his tone, and my hackles rose.

"No one." I stood, shoving my phone into the back pocket of my jeans and walked to the kitchen. Aiden followed, his boots thudding on the floor.

"Scarlett, what aren't you telling me?" He gripped my arm and spun me around.

"Get your hand off me." I glanced down at his hand and back up to his sparking eyes.

Aiden stepped back and raised his hands in a gesture of surrender. "Why won't you tell me who it was?"

"Because it was Sadie," I said, exasperated. "And it shouldn't matter. We aren't dating. We aren't a couple. And even if we were, it wouldn't give you license to control me."

He stepped back as if I'd struck him. "When have I ever controlled you or anything you've done?"

"You controlled every aspect of this move," I snapped.

"If I'd controlled anything about it, you wouldn't have moved here in the first place." He was inches from my face, his own red with anger. "Hell, you wouldn't have left four years ago, and I wouldn't have missed out on time with my daughter." The more he spoke, the angrier he became. He stalked away from me and paced for a minute before he came to a halt in front of me again. "Don't mistake caring for control. I'm not your psycho ex."

I winced at his words. He was right. He wasn't Justin. I rubbed my temples as a headache formed. "Look, I'm tired and I'm sure you are too. Let's just call it a night and we can talk tomorrow."

"Whatever you want." He stormed into the living room, snatched up his keys and opened the door. Before he stepped out, he said, "Make no mistake, Scarlett. You're controlling this entire situation. I haven't had a say in anything since you walked out on me."

The door slammed as he left, and the thud of his boots as he walked down the steps punctuated his exit. My feet were glued to the same spot until he peeled out of the driveway and sped down the road. Once I was sure he was gone, I armed the security system, exactly the way he'd shown me, and trudged up the stairs to go to bed.

I checked on Tillie before going to my room. She was curled up under the covers, oblivious to the emotional turmoil that felt supercharged in the tiny house. Satisfied that she was okay, I went to my room, leaving the door open a crack, in case she needed anything during the night. I stripped down to my panties and crawled under the covers.

As I lay there, I couldn't help but wonder about how different things could have been if I hadn't left when I'd found out I was pregnant. Would Aiden and I still be together? Would Justin have left us alone? Would Tillie have siblings? So many possibilities and I'd thrown them down the drain like spoiled milk.

I rolled onto my side and punched my pillow, trying to get comfortable.

Face it, Scar. You haven't been comfortable in four years and nine months.

16

AIDEN

"Go away!"

The incessant pounding on my front door was pissing me off. I rolled over and picked up my cell phone to check the time. Seven-thirty. Too fucking early, but the banging wouldn't stop. I rolled out of bed and threw my boxer briefs on before going to yell at whoever had woken me up.

"I'm coming. Jesus, stop with the knocking," I yelled as I yanked open the door and came face to face with Griffin and Micah. "Do you have any idea what fucking time it is?"

"Do you talk like that around Tillie?" Micah shouldered his way past me and went straight to the kitchen. "And it's not that early. You should be used to it, what with Tillie and Scarlett being here as long as they were."

"They're not fucking here now, are they?"

I hadn't moved away from the open door and Griffin stood just inside, arms crossed over his chest, smug grin in place. Realizing that they weren't going to leave me alone, I slammed the door and leaned back against it. The sounds of

Micah making coffee drifted to me, and Griffin had yet to move.

"What the hell's so funny?" I shot daggers at Griffin and stomped past him.

"Dude, you need to get a grip. It's been less than twelve hours, and you're gonna see her tonight." Griffin accepted the mug that Micah handed him.

"If your damn wives hadn't—"

"Don't," Micah warned. "You're not going to blame this on our wives. All they're guilty of is being friends with Scarlett." He lifted his cup to his lips, but before he took a sip, he said, "Now go put some damn clothes on."

I glanced down but didn't budge. "Scarlett would still be here if it weren't for them encouraging her idea to get a place of her own."

"Keep telling yourself that if it makes you feel better." Griffin twisted a chair around and straddled it. "But if I were you, I'd take this opportunity and use the fuck out of it."

"What are you talking about?" I eyed him suspiciously. He was my best friend and always had my back, so I really wanted to know what he had to say, despite my bad attitude.

"Go cover your cranky ass and I'll tell you." His eyebrows raised in a challenging manner.

I went and threw on a pair of sweats and a T-shirt. When I re-entered the kitchen, both men were seated at the table, talking about God only knew what.

"I'm dressed." I straddled the chair at the end of the table so I could see both of them. "Care to enlighten me on what great opportunity you think it is I have?"

Micah was the first to respond. "Dude, she could've left like she did before. But she didn't. She's still in town because that's where she wants to be."

"But what if Jus—"

"Stop," Griffin spoke up. "Aiden, we're damn good at our jobs. She's got a top of the line security system, and it's linked to your cell phone. Jackson put out an APB on him so if he even so much as breathes within the county limits, he's toast. You're never this wound up over a case. Trust yourself, man. Trust *us*."

"I do trust you. All of you. And I know I can keep her safe, keep them *both* safe." I clenched my fists on the table. "But you both know as well as I do that she's not just any client."

"And neither were Sadie and Brie." Micah stood to refill his coffee mug. When he held out the pot to refill ours, I shook my head. After replacing the carafe, he stood next to the table. "Listen, I talked to Sadie and got her take on this whole Scarlett and Tillie living on their own thing."

"And?"

"And, I think she and Brie were onto something." Micah glanced at Griffin and Griffin nodded for him to continue. "This is the perfect way for you to win Scarlett over. Get to know her. Really know her."

"We have a fucking daughter. I know her." I shoved up out of the chair, and it tipped back and banged against the edge of the table.

"True, but apparently she doesn't see it that way." Griffin stood up and grabbed my shoulders to stop me from storming off. "You have to show her that you're in this for all the right reasons."

"What the hell is that supposed to mean?" I shrugged him off. "Of course I'm in it for the right reasons."

"Does she know that?" Micah stepped in front of me.

That was a damn good question. How could she not know? I'd dropped everything when I'd gotten the call from the hospital and found out I had a daughter. I'd stepped up and provided a place for them to stay. I'd been there every step of the way since she was attacked. I loved them.

But does she know that?

Fuck!

"I can see you just figured it out." Griffin laughed as he deposited his now empty coffee cup in the sink.

"I don't know what else I can do, though. I don't know what more she wants from me to know that I'm in it for the long haul. That I love her." I sat back down with a thump.

"Dude, you've gotta tell her."

"More importantly, you've gotta show her." Micah slapped me on the back as he and Griffin walked out and left me to my own thoughts.

They were right. This wasn't the ideal setup as far as I was concerned, but it was a damn good chance for me to prove myself to her. All of a sudden, what I had to do became crystal clear. Not only did I have to ensure their safety...

I had to woo Scarlett.

"Where's Tillie?"

I'd arrived at Scarlett's rental with a bottle of wine and a bouquet of flowers in hand. She'd asked me over for dinner, to talk, but the look on her face when she'd opened the door told me everything I needed to know. She hadn't expected me to treat it like a real date. A proper date.

"She's in her room playing." Scarlett put the flowers in a glass cup and set them on the island in the kitchen. "I'll call her down when dinner is ready."

"Okay." I shoved my hands in the pockets of my jeans.

Nervousness had crept in the moment I'd realized what I needed to do, and it had only intensified when I got here. There was no room for error.

"What's gotten into you?" Scarlett moved from the counter and stood in front of me, hand on her cocked hip.

How did I explain to her that I wanted to date her? We'd

skipped some pretty critical steps in the relationship department, and I'd never struggled to tell her exactly what I wanted or what I was feeling. But it hadn't mattered as much as it did now.

"I'm nervous." Honestly was the best policy, and if I wanted to prove to her that I wanted to be with her and that it wasn't just because of Tillie, I should probably stick to the tried and true.

"Bullshit." She rolled her eyes and flapped her hand at me. "You're never nervous. You're the most confident person I've ever met."

I drew in a deep breath and dove in headfirst. "Correction. I *was* confident." Her eyes widened and lips parted. I held my hand up to silence her impending interruption. "I was. I'll admit that. But then you left."

"I know." She dropped her head to stare at the floor for a long minute. When she raised it, her eyes locked with mine. "I'm sorry I left the way I did. I'm sorry I kept Tillie from you. I'm just… sorry."

"I'm not telling you this for an apology, although it's appreciated." I took a tentative step toward her, and when she didn't shy away from me, I stepped even closer. "Ya know, it occurred to me today that there are a lot of things we don't know about each other."

"It did?" Her eyes narrowed as if trying to figure out what my game was, but she was destined to be disappointed as far as that was concerned. No games here.

"Yeah, it did." I reached out and grabbed her hands and brought them to my mouth to kiss her palms. "But I want you to know everything. So," I took a deep breath and exhaled. "I think we should get to know each other. Spend time together, just the two of us." I placed a finger to her lips when she tried to speak. "And as a family. Tillie is a part of the equation no matter what happens with us, but I want you to know that we can be... no, we *are* more than just parents together."

"But how do you know that? How can you be sure?" Confusion swirled in her eyes, along with a hint of desperation.

I shrugged. "I just know."

"Aiden, that's not good enough." She pulled her hands out of my grasp and stepped back. "I'm a mother now. I have respo—"

"And I'm a father. Last time I checked, to the same little girl." I was determined to make her see that we belonged together, and she was just as determined to resist. "If you ask me, that's a good place to start."

"To start what?" She narrowed her eyes suspiciously.

"Dating."

"You want to date me?"

"Sugar, I want a lot more than that, but yeah, for now, I'll settle for dating."

A blush crept into her cheeks, and a second later I realized that it wasn't a blush. It was anger.

"That's just it!" She stomped toward me and thrust a finger at my chest. "I don't want you to settle. I don't want you to be a part of our lives out of, of, of some crazy notion that you *have* to be!"

I wrapped my fingers around her wrist and tugged her to my chest. My arms went around her waist, and when she struggled, I tightened my hold.

"I'm not here because I have to be." I leaned down and placed a kiss on her forehead before peering into her eyes. "I'm here because I want to be. And it's not 'settling'. With you, it's never settling. Just give me a chance to prove it to you."

"But what if—"

"Just try." I maintained my hold on her but lowered my mouth to her ear. "All I ask is that you try."

She shivered as my breath skated over her skin, but she didn't speak.

"Scarlett?"

"Huh?"

"Can you try?" When she still didn't say anything, I added a condition that would only make it harder on me. "Give me a month. One month to show you that I'm here for all the right reasons. If, at the end of that month, you still want me to leave you alone, I will."

"One month?" Her forehead rested on my chest, so her voice was muffled.

"Yep."

"And you promise you'll walk away?"

I had no idea how to answer that because honestly? I didn't think I could walk away from her. But if that's what she needed to hear than I'd say it. I'd say anything to get her to agree.

"If you truly don't want me, yes. I promise."

My heart broke at those words, but I shoved some emotional super glue into the cracks and ignored it.

17

SCARLETT

*W*hen Aiden said he promised, I decided to take him at his word. One thing he'd never done was lie to me.

"Fine." I pushed away from him and wrung my hands in front of me. "I'll try."

Breath whooshed past his lips, and his shoulders sunk as if the weight of the entire world had just been lifted off of them.

"Sugar, you won't regret this." He smiled and when he did, I remembered why it had been so hard to leave the first time around. If my body's reaction was any indication, this time would be so much worse.

"We'll see about that," I mumbled as I turned toward the sound of the oven timer.

When I walked into the kitchen, Aiden followed. I opened the oven door and sighed in relief at the perfectly crisp edges of the lasagna, not that Aiden cared about perfection. He would eat pretty much anything I put in front of him, but I'd wanted to impress him.

He stepped up behind me and took the potholders out of

my hands and lifted the pan out to set it on top of the stove. Steam billowed from the gooey cheese, and the smells that filled the room made my mouth water.

"That looks delicious." I leaned over and took a whiff, practically drooling in his appreciation. "I didn't know you could cook."

"Picked up a lot of things the last few years." I turned from him and walked toward the stairs to get Tillie.

"I'll get her." Aiden rushed to my side and stopped short of the first step. "If that's okay?"

"Um, yeah, it's fine." I turned away from him and listened to his heavy footsteps on the stairs.

Even though he was on a different level of the house, his deep voice filtered down to me, mixed in with Tillie's higher-pitched one. I listened to their banter, and when the sound of them coming downstairs registered, I rushed to finish setting the table.

Plates and silverware were already in place, but the drinks were still missing. I grabbed the milk and a sippy cup for Tillie and two beers for Aiden and me. I didn't drink a lot, but I needed one tonight.

Supper was an active affair. Tillie talked non-stop about nothing in particular, and Aiden was tuned in to every single word. I watched him interact with her and the way that Tillie came out of her shell with him, it made me happy. Genuinely happy. But if there was one thing I knew about happiness, it was that it tended to be short-lived.

"Dinner was great, Scarlett." Aiden tossed his napkin onto his empty plate and pushed his chair back to stand. "I'll clean up. Why don't you go give Tillie her bath?"

He started to clear the table, not waiting for a response.

"Mommy, can I haf a bubble bath?"

"Sure, baby."

I went through the motions of giving Tillie her bath and

getting her settled for the night. She loved bubble baths and also making a mess, so when she was tucked in and asleep, I returned to the bathroom to clean up.

When I stepped through the threshold, my breath caught. Aiden was bent over, tight jean-clad ass on display, picking up the towels off the floor.

"I was gonna get that."

Aiden stood up so fast he smacked his head on the towel bar. "Fuck!" He rubbed the spot where his skull smarted and whirled on me. "You scared me."

"I'm sorry." I chewed on my bottom lip to keep from laughing.

"You think that's funny?" He scrunched his face up in mock anger, but his own laughter danced in his eyes. "Huh?"

I shook my head as he advanced on me. The closer he got, the more my laughter died and heat pooled in my belly.

"Sugar, you better run."

He reached out to tickle me, something he used to do a lot, and I bolted. Turned and ran down the steps into the living room. He was right on my heels, and when I rounded the couch, he scooped me up and tossed me down onto the new furniture.

"You're gonna pay for that." He braced his arms on either side of me and leaned in close. "You must be held accountable for your actions."

"My actions?" The question was barely audible because of the lust I was experiencing. I was fairly certain I'd enjoy his version of 'holding me accountable' but was I ready for that?

"Yeah." He pressed a kiss to my cheek. "Your actions." He trailed his lips to my neck and pressed them to my ear. "Sexy as fuck." He drew my lobe into his mouth and sucked.

"Aiden?" His name was a whispered plea. For what, I had no idea.

"Shhh. Just feel." His breath on my skin sent shockwaves through me.

He lowered his body onto mine, and his cock rubbed against me through our jeans. The contact was like ice water to my hormones. Sure, I wanted him. That was never our problem. But I also wanted to make sure that there was more than just sex between us, and if he insisted on this whole month thing then I was going to take it seriously.

"Aiden?" I turned my head away from him and pushed against his chest. "Aiden, stop."

That one word was all it took. He reared up and locked eyes with mine. His breathing was heavy, his weight, heavier.

"Sugar, you keep rocking into me like that I'm liable to think you don't really want me to stop."

Damn. He was right. I hadn't even realized I was doing it so I forced myself to lie still. He chuckled at me before pushing away and sitting up.

"I'm so—"

"Don't. Please don't say you're sorry." He thrust a frustrated hand through his hair. "You don't ever need to apologize for that."

"'Kay. Thanks."

I sat up and hugged a pillow to my chest. Aiden turned and brought a bent leg onto the couch as he faced me. He reached out to brush my hair out of my face, and I leaned into the contact.

"You like it when I touch you."

It wasn't a question, but I nodded anyway. I didn't trust myself to speak.

"But you stopped me." He tilted his head. "Why?"

"Because sex…"

"Sex, what?" he asked when I trailed off.

I blew out a breath. "Sex has never been a problem for us.

I know we're great together… in bed. What I want to know is if we're good together out of bed."

"We're perfect together no matter what, but I get it." He stood and walked across the room to stare at the picture I had framed of Tillie. When he turned back around, there was a determination in his eyes that wasn't there before. "I think we need to focus on talking right now."

Shit.

I wasn't ready for that either.

"What do you want to talk about?" I asked, hoping he wouldn't suggest the last four years.

He must have sensed my anxiety because he surprised me. "How about you tell me about your childhood?"

My eyes widened, but a smile tugged at my lips. "I can do that." I stood up and went to the kitchen to pour us both a glass of wine.

When I returned to the living room, Aiden was still standing in the same spot, so I handed him his glass.

"Thanks." He lifted it to his lips and took a healthy sip.

"So, my childhood, huh?" I tilted my head at him as if trying to determine his angle. I wasn't going to look a gift horse in the mouth, but I was curious as to why he didn't start with the harder stuff. It was what he did, after all.

"Yep. Figure we'll get to the rest eventually." His crooked grin was perfection to me and immediately eased my nerves. It always had.

"Well, there's nothing too exciting." I sat back down on the sofa and curled my legs under me. "I already told you that I was an Army brat. My dad was stationed all over the place, so I've been practically everywhere. It was fun, for the most part." I paused as I thought back over all the moves to new cities and foreign countries, all the friends I was never able to keep. Sadness crept in at that thought, but I pushed it back.

"I still can't believe your dad was in the Army." Aiden sat down on the other end of the couch and peered at me. "You never said anything about that when you came for help before."

"He's still in the Army." I waved my hand like that was beside the point. "By the time I met you, it was… a sore spot." I took another sip of the white wine and savored it as it slid down my throat. "When I turned eighteen, he was transferred overseas. We'd just returned stateside two years prior, and I didn't want to go again. I wanted to go to college, make friends, live life like a normal eighteen-year-old would. So, I pitched a fit." I shrugged and dropped my eyes, unable to bear the disappointment I'd see in his. He was a military man just like my father. He wouldn't understand someone who wanted nothing more to do with it.

"Ah, makes sense." My head whipped up to lock eyes with him. He smiled at my shocked expression. "Scarlett, you were just a kid. I get it. You didn't choose that life. Your dad did."

"Yes, well, turns out I should have listened to all of his protests about me staying behind." I drew my lips between my teeth. It seemed I'd managed to get us exactly where I hadn't wanted the conversation to lead.

"Sugar, it's okay. It's not like I don't know that something happened at some point to have you running to my door." He tilted his head and narrowed his eyes, as if something just occurred to him. "I do have one question though."

"Only one?"

"No, actually. I want to hear everything you want to tell me. I want to know all about the little girl who grew up on Army bases around the world. But for now, I'll settle on the one."

"Okay."

"Back when you first came to us for help, why us? Why

not go to your parents? It sounds like, if he was overseas, that may have been the safer option."

Of course he'd ask that. I'd asked myself the same thing a million times. Problem was, no matter how stupid my decision may have been, I kept circling back to one thing: I wouldn't have had Tillie if I had gone to my parents, and I couldn't regret that. I stood and started to pace.

"When I met Justin, things were great. I was on top of the world. A freshman in college, making friends that I wouldn't have to say goodbye to within months. I had a life." I stopped pacing in front of the coffee table and set my wine glass down. When I straightened, I crossed my arms over my chest as if to shield myself from the rest of the details. "But as you know, things changed."

"You don't have to keep going if you don't want to." He gave me an out, but I knew he was praying I wouldn't take it.

"That's where you're wrong. I know this is all stuff you need to know, especially if I have a chance in hell of you protecting us." I glanced toward the stairs, letting my mind's eye take me to Tillie's room as if to make sure she was still tucked in, safe. "I just don't like the picture it paints of me."

Aiden stood and came to stand behind me. His arms came around me, offering comfort.

"The BRB can protect you no matter what you tell me. *I* can protect you. Both of you."

I soaked up the heat he provided, let it seep into my bones and warm me from the inside out. I took a deep breath but still no more words came out.

Aiden loosened his hold and stepped around me, never completely breaking contact. When he was standing in front of me, his hands cupped my face, and he bent at the knees to bring himself to eye level.

"Whatever he did, it wasn't your fault."

"I know that." A humorless laugh escaped me. "I'm not

one of those girls who blames herself for every bad thing that's ever happened. I didn't deserve what he did. I didn't ask for it." My eyes slid closed and I whispered, "But neither did Tillie."

"Open those beautiful eyes for me. I want you to see me when I tell you this." I slowly opened my eyes, and his burned into my soul. "Good girl." He smiled. "You're right. You didn't deserve it. And no, neither did Tillie. But you can't change it. No one can, although God knows I wish I could. But that's not how life works. All you can do now is get pissed and let that carry you through. And know that I'm here no matter what."

"How can you say that?" He was right. I needed to be pissed. Pissed was a hell of a lot easier to deal with than confused and scared. "You don't even know everything. And what you do know doesn't exactly make me woman of the year."

I pushed out of his hold and started to pace again. I rubbed my forehead as I tried to form a coherent thought to make him understand that, while I didn't deserve what Justin did, I also didn't deserve Aiden's forgiveness. Not after keeping his daughter from him. That was unforgivable.

"Stop." His voice seemed to reverberate off the walls, and I halted, facing him. "Look, Scarlett, I'm not going to lie and say I'm not still angry about you keeping Tillie from me. Hell, I don't know if I'll ever not be a little angry about it. If you knew—" He slammed his mouth shut and then took a deep breath to calm whatever was raging through him. "There's a part of me that wants to hate you for not telling me about her. For leaving the way you did." He rubbed a hand over his chest, as if he was physically in pain. "But there's a bigger part of me," he thumped his chest with his fist, "right here, that doesn't give a fuck about any of it. You're it for me. You and Tillie."

"Aiden, please don't say that. What if…?"

"What? What if you have to leave again?" I nodded, solemnly. "Sugar, you try to leave again and I'll track your ass down and drag you back if it's the last thing I do."

I laughed, a watery laugh, and that's when I realized that I'd been crying. He tentatively stepped toward me, and when I didn't move away, he closed the distance and wrapped his arms around me, pulling my head toward his chest.

"You never answered my question."

"What question?"

"Why did you come to us and not your parents?"

I blew out a breath. There was no turning back now. "Justin threatened them. My parents, I mean. They knew what was going on. I may have not wanted to go back overseas, but I never kept anything from them. When I'd made the decision to run, my dad didn't like it but he knew how stubborn I could be. I made it clear to him that I wasn't going overseas so he gave me the location of a place I'd be safe."

"Then why, for God's sake did you come to Indiana? It makes no sense. Your Army dad tells you about a safe place and you don't go there. *Why?*"

I tipped my head back so he could see me when I answered. "I did. He sent me to the BRB. He sent me to you."

18

AIDEN

He sent me to you.

What the fuck? When Scarlett had uttered those words, my world rocked on its axis yet again. I'd demanded that she explain, and she'd tried, but she wasn't the one who could give me all of the answers.

It had taken all of my self-control not to track down the information when I left Scarlett's house, but it had been too late. Problem with waiting was it gave me all night to think up all kinds of worst-case betrayal scenarios.

I cut Calypso's engine, dropped the kickstand and swung my leg over the bike. I glanced up and down the street and noticed that there wasn't much traffic in town. Not that there ever was. That's why we picked this place. Well, part of the reason.

When I pulled open the door to the station, I was greeted by the receptionist.

"Where is he?" I slammed my fists down on her desk and immediately, a few deputies stood, clearly sensing my fury.

"I, uh, he's out on a call." Her eyes shifted nervously. "Can I give him a message for you?"

"Yeah." I shoved off the desk and backed toward the door. "Tell him he better get his ass to my place as soon as he can. He's got some *questions* to answer."

"Will do, Mr. Winters. Have a good day," she called out to my back as the door closed behind me.

I climbed back on Calypso, gunned the engine and tore out of town. If Jackson couldn't answer my questions right now then maybe my brothers would know something. The thought of them keeping something like this from me ate at me, and I hated that I doubted them, but I had to know.

I slid the bike to a stop in Micah's driveway, noticing Griffin's bike parked next to the garage. Good, kill two birds with one stone.

I didn't bother knocking, but there was no one in the living room when I entered. Voices carried from the kitchen, so I stormed into the room and all eyes turned to me.

"What the fuck, Aiden?" Micah rose from his chair and stepped up to me. "Since when—"

My fist connected with his nose, and his head flew back, blood spurting. Griffin and Brie were out of their seats so fast, holding me back as I tried to advance on Micah again.

"Dude, what the hell are you doing?" Griffin's voice was muffled, all the blood rushing in my ears drowning out coherent sound. "Calm the fuck down."

I struggled against their holds but to no avail. Griffin on my right and Brie on my left, they held me in place as I watched Micah wipe his nose with the back of his hand.

"Let him go," Micah said.

"If we do, are you gonna try to clean his clock?" There was laughter in Brie's voice as she addressed me, but there was nothing funny about this situation.

"Depends," I grated out between clenched teeth.

"On?" Micah asked.

"On what you can tell me about General Runyon." I watched his eyes closely, looking for any sign of a lie.

"Who the fuck is General Runyon?" Griffin asked, sounding genuinely confused. At least he didn't seem to have held anything back from me.

"Care to tell him?" I tilted my head at Micah, hoping he'd give me an excuse to unload more of my rage.

"I would if I had any fucking clue." He grabbed me by the shirt and shook me. "But I don't. You can either believe that or not. Quite frankly, I've got half a mind to kick your ass to the fucking curb for this little stunt."

What the hell are you doing, questioning the people who have been nothing but solid since day one?

My entire body deflated of anger, and I hung my head. Griff and Brie let me go and stepped around to stand next to Micah. I wasn't looking at them, too ashamed to, but I could feel their stares burning a hole into the top of my head.

"If you're finished slinging accusations, maybe you'd like to sit down and try actually talking to us." Micah's voice had calmed a little, which shouldn't surprise me because he was like that. Forgiving, stoic, *loyal*.

"Yeah, fine." Even though I felt bad for barging in here like I did and cracking my pres's nose, I still had a chip on my shoulder.

When all of us were seated, silence prevailed. I glanced at the faces of three of the most important people in my life. That's when I noticed someone missing.

"Where's Sadie?" I looked to Micah for the answer, and his eyes narrowed.

"You're damn lucky she's not here." He shook his head at me. "Had you pulled that shit with her here, this would have gone down a completely different way. Whatever you take away from this, let that be it. You will *not* lose your temper in front of my wife. Do you hear me?"

"Yeah. Yeah, I hear ya." Shame flooded my system. I was better than this. I was the fun one. The class clown. Keeping my cool was what had made me so damn good as a Navy Seal. And I'd managed to throw that all away in the short time that Scarlett had been back. *Fuck.*

"Why don't you tell us why you're here? What's got your panties all twisted around your ankles?" I glanced at Brie while she spoke, and she smiled. Leave it to her to try and make a joke out of it.

"Who's General Runyon?" Griffin asked and as the question passed his lips a light entered his eyes. "Wait. Runyon? As in the same last name as Scarlett?"

"Oh yeah. General Tom Runyon is her father." Griffin was pulling out his phone, no doubt to look up whatever information he could on the General. He'd dig deeper on his computer later. "Apparently the good General knows Jackson."

"Okay. I'm still not real clear on why you came in here swinging." Micah stood and grabbed a few beers from the fridge.

"I'm getting to that." I took the bottle Micah offered and chugged down a healthy swig. When I slammed the bottle back on the table, all eyes returned to me. "Last night, Scarlett told me that when she came here four years ago, she did because her father sent her here." They all stared, questions in their eyes at where I was going with this. "Jackson told the General about us."

"That makes no sense." Griffin narrowed his eyes as if searching his brain for a way to make it make sense. "How does Jackson know the General? And why the hell would you take a chunk out of Micah because of it?"

I glanced at Micah. "I'm sorry about that. It's just, when Scarlett told me all of this, my mind wandered. I haven't been able to figure out a single scenario where Jackson knows the Runyon's so my thoughts went to the next logical thing. You guys." I glanced around the table, taking in all of them. "I guess I just figured you'd been keeping something from me."

"I'm going to assume that most of the blood required to use your brain at its full capacity is pumping to your dick and let this one go. But fuck, man, when have we ever not been one hundred percent honest with you?"

Brie snorted at Micah's comment, but when his gaze cut to her, she schooled her features and mouthed 'sorry'.

"Right? I don't know what the hell I was thinking." I shrugged. "I wasn't. That's the only excuse I've got. I went to the station to confront Jackson before coming here, but he was out. I demanded that he come to my place when he got back."

"What's your plan for when he shows?" Brie asked.

"Honestly, no fucking clue." I stood to throw my bottle in the trash. "But he has some explaining to do. He was already on thin ice with me but now? How the fuck am I supposed to let this go?"

"Maybe it's not as bad as it seems. What does Scarlett say about all of this?"

"Just that her dad told her about us and that we could protect her. She said her dad didn't give her many details, just that he had a friend named Jackson who was a sheriff and he vouched for us."

"That's good though, right? I mean, if he vouched for us then I'm not so sure he did anything wrong." Brie was trying to find the good in this. Jackson had been a big part of her rescue, and she had a soft spot for the guy.

"He didn't tell me! This whole time, the last four years, he *knew* I was looking for her. He fucking knew and never said a word about any of this. He may have known where she was!"

My temper rose and Micah stood, placing himself next to

me and a hand on my forearm, as if physically warning me to chill out.

"Let's not jump to conclusions," he said.

"Little late for that, don't ya think?" Griffin huffed out before standing to throw his empty bottle away. "Besides, I'm with Aiden on this one." My gaze cut to him in surprise. "Jackson needs to answer for this. But he's the fucking Sheriff. You can't cold cock him the way you did Micah."

"We'll all talk to Jackson when he's here. Until then, let's talk about what we know for sure. Fill us in on anything Scarlett's told you about the last four years. We'll start trying to track the bastard down who put her in the hospital." Micah had given his orders and we weren't to question them. To be honest, I didn't want to. It hadn't felt good to be suspicious of him, and I needed his authority to ground me just then.

"I've got a name. Justin Chalmers. I looked into him a bit last night when I got home from Scarlett's house. He's got a pretty nasty history. Burglary, assault, check fraud." I looked at Griffin, who'd started inputting all of this info into the notes app on his phone. "But the icing on the cake? Dishonorably discharged from the Army two and a half years before Scarlett showed up on my doorstep."

"And you didn't think to lead with that?" Micah shook his head at me, clearly baffled with my course of action.

"Saving the best for last?" I was joking, sort of. The logical part of my brain knew I should have taken that bit of information and ran with it, but as Micah pointed out, I wasn't firing on all cylinders.

"Does Scarlett know about his connection to the Army?" Griffin asked.

"She said he was an Army brat, like her, but I don't think she knows he was actually in the Army himself. If she did, she hasn't mentioned it. And I'm not sure I want her to know. I mean, the way she talked about her family? She loves them and if they kept information from her, it'd kill her."

"Aiden, you can't keep this from her." Brie gripped my arm. "It's not like you're suggesting that her father is behind everything that happened to her, right?"

"Of course not. But…"

"But nothing." Brie let go of me. "Trust me. You can't keep anything from her. Not if you expect to have a future with her and Tillie. You lie to her now, you can kiss that goodbye."

I shoved a shaky hand through my hair. "You're right. I know you are. I just want to protect her. I don't want to be the one to make her sad. And this douchebag's connection to the fucking military?" I shook my head. "I don't know how to process that, ya know?"

"Aiden, not everyone with military connections are good people. I know it fucking sucks because we bleed red, white and blue. But that's life. You do the best you can and hopefully hook up with the right people, connect with the good ones. You did that. We all did." Micah paused to encompass Griffin and Brie. "Sounds like this Justin guy didn't. Which sucks balls for him because now he has us hunting him down. He'll regret his choices. We'll make sure of it. And something tells me that's exactly why her father sent her to us. So we could dole out justice in a way he couldn't."

"Yeah, I bet he never thought it would result in a baby. Or his daughter living on the run for four years."

"Probably not but there's nothing you can do about that now." Micah turned to Griffin and Brie. "Can you two go back to your place and dig up whatever info you can on Justin?" When they both nodded, he returned his attention back to me. "You and I will head to your place and wait on Jackson. I agree that he needs to give us some answers, but I'd prefer as little bloodshed as possible."

"Fine. Let's go."

I walked out of the house, not waiting for anyone to follow. As I drove Calypso to my place, a strong desire to change course and head to Scarlett's rose up. I wanted to take them both away from here, away from a betrayal I had no idea how it would play out. Take them to some place safe, where no evil could touch them. But I didn't. Instead, I pulled into my driveway and pulled out my phone to send a quick text that gave away nothing of the internal battle I was facing.

Me: Had fun last night. Can't wait to see you again.

Three dots appeared and disappeared just as quickly. I knew it would do me no good to watch for her response, so I shoved my phone back in my pocket and entered my house. Micah arrived a few minutes later, and when he walked through the door, my cell beeped. I glanced at the screen and smiled for the first time all day.

Scarlett: Me too. Maybe we could go for a ride later?

Me: Anything you want, Sugar. Pick you up at 7. I'll bring a babysitter.

∽

Two hours.

That's how long Micah and I had to wait for Jackson. When he arrived, I wanted to tear into him, but Micah kept me from doing anything stupid and getting arrested. A person can assault the sheriff only so many times and get away with it.

"What the hell was so important that you came into the

station and got shitty with my staff?" Jackson's level of anger didn't even come close to matching mine.

"I want some fucking answers, that's what." I stepped up to him, and Micah's hand on my shoulder pulled me back.

"What Aiden is trying to say is that he was given some information that might lead someone to believe you've been keeping something from him." Micah's tone was much calmer than the words suggested. He was one of the most loyal people I knew, and it didn't sit well with him to think that he, or anyone else, had been lied to. The difference between him and I, though, was he'd mellowed with marriage and wanted all of the facts before slinging accusations.

Jackson's eyes narrowed, as if trying to determine what information Micah was talking about. He was good, I'd give him that.

"How do you know General Runyon?" I was done waiting.

"Oh." Jackson's shoulders slumped and his face fell. "I served under him for a short time."

"Go on."

"Shit." He cracked his knuckles before crossing his arms over his chest. "Okay, I served for four years, didn't re-enlist because of personal reasons. General Runyon saw me through some dark times, helped me get into law enforcement as a civilian. We stayed in touch." He shrugged as if it wasn't a big deal. As if there wasn't more to the story, when clearly there was.

"Why is Scarlett under the impression that her father sent her to us four years ago based on your recommendation?" Micah had a way of putting things much more politely than I would have.

"Because he did."

"What the fuck, Jackson? You knew her when she came

here? And didn't help. Not only that, but for the last four years, you *knew* where she was and said *nothing*."

"How many times do I have to tell you guys? I have a job to do, and sometimes it doesn't involve me telling you everything. Hell, most of the time you don't know what I do. I'm the law here, not you."

Jackson turned to go to the door, but I gripped his arm and spun him back around.

"Don't you dare wal—"

"Aiden!" I glanced over my shoulder at Micah's voice. "Let him go. If he doesn't want to help, then we can't force him." He refocused on Jackson. "He's right. He's the law and we're not. I've still got connections in the military. Maybe General Runyon would be interested in knowing that his *good friend* Jackson isn't using all available resources to keep his daughter and granddaughter safe."

"Threats, Mic? Really?" Jackson arched an eyebrow. He wouldn't back down easily, but he knew when he was had.

"No threat here, Sheriff. Just fact." Micah let go of me and took my place in front of Jackson, poking a finger at his chest. "I don't appreciate the fact that you not only lied to Aiden, but to me, as well. We've done nothing to deserve that. But that's beside the point. We now have to protect a woman who was beaten nearly to death, and your actions didn't help the situation. You have to live with that. Not us."

"Jesus, do you really have that low of an opinion of me?"

"I didn't. Fuck, Jackson." Micah shoved a hand through his hair. "I don't know what the hell to think. But you're not helping any by playing things so close to the vest."

Jackson squared his shoulders and drew a deep breath. "I'll give you the information I have, but you're bound to be disappointed." He turned to me. "Aiden, I didn't keep anything from you." When I raised my brows, he chuckled.

"Well, not as much as you think, at least. Can I get a whiskey? I'm gonna need it if I'm spilling my guts."

Jackson didn't wait for an answer before shoving his way past Micah and me to head to the kitchen. I briefly looked at Micah and he shrugged. I got Jackson his whiskey, and we sat at the table. It was silent for several minutes, other than the sound of my racing heart. When Jackson drained his glass and slammed it on the table, he leaned forward and finally spoke.

"Like I said, I was in the Army and served under General Runyon. Tom was a hard-ass, but he actually gave a damn about his men." While he talked, he stared into his empty glass, not once making eye contact. "Just before I re-upped, my son was born."

His words triggered a memory of he and I arguing on the side of the road. So, that's what he'd meant when he said he was a father too. Right before he lost his shit.

"I didn't know you were married." I didn't know he was a father either, not really, but at least he'd hinted at it before.

"Well, I was. Until I wasn't." Still no eye contact.

"What the hell does that mean, Jackson? You're saying a whole hell of a lot without saying a fucking thing."

"I'd just gotten back to my tent after a long shift, and the General came in. Said a call came in that my wife and son had died." He raised his head and cold, hard eyes stared at me. "Murdered by a thug looking for drugs." Those hard eyes became glassy, and I shifted in my seat. I'd wanted answers, not this. "My mother-in-law had been staying at our house because she'd just had surgery. Turns out even thugs draw the line at murdering the elderly. But not young women. Not little boys."

"Fuck, man. I don't even know what to say." Guilt ate at me, but I pushed it down. What happened to Jackson was terrible, but it didn't change anything. Not yet, at least. "Still not real clear what this has to do with the Runyon's."

"I'm getting there." He stood to refill his whiskey and drank it down before continuing. "The General made sure that I had time to grieve. He made sure that I was okay. I was young, stupid, a real dick after all of that, but he kept me going. Turned all of my anger into something positive. When my time was up, I left. He kept tabs on me, helped me along the way, made sure that I continued to use my emotions for good."

"Sounds like a good man."

"He was. Is. Anyway, he called me four years ago and asked if I knew of anywhere his daughter could go to lay low for a while. Said she had a stalker. He wouldn't give me much information. Said it was safer that way. Scarlett showed up, and if you'll recall, that was the same time everything happened with Sadie."

"That doesn't mean we couldn't handle anything else. We were working other cases. Besides, I'm more concerned with the fact that you could have told me where Scarlett was the last four years."

"I didn't know where she was! Not until I got the call from the hospital." He held up his hand to stop me when my lips parted. "And before you even ask, I had no idea about Tillie. I haven't talked to the General in a while, but whenever I did, he never said a word. I'm sorry she got hurt. I'm sorry you missed out on time with your daughter, but man, there was nothing to tell."

"Let's say you're telling us the truth—"

"I am!"

"Fine. You are. Doesn't mean we have to like it."

"No, you don't. And I'll give you any information I have so you can do this right. So your family is safe."

"How noble of you," I scoffed. I understood that he didn't hide much from me, but the bitterness was still there.

"It's not noble. I have a feeling the BRB is the only chance those two have of staying safe."

"You're not going to help?"

"I will for a bit, but there's going to be a new Sheriff soon."

Micah and I came out of our chairs so fast that they almost toppled over.

"What do you mean? Where the fuck are you going?" I demanded.

"It hasn't been announced yet, but I've accepted a position with the FBI. I'll still be somewhat local, based out of Indianapolis."

"Would you have told us if we hadn't confronted you today?"

"Of course I would have. I was planning on telling my staff first, but you blew that all to hell. I'll put in a good word for you with my replacement, but your free reign will likely end with me. So I suggest we get this thing with Scarlett wrapped up quickly." Jackson focused on me. "Something tells me you won't let the boundaries of the law stop you from doing whatever it takes. You can be mad at me all you want, Aiden, but you're going to need me and you know it."

Damn if he wasn't right.

19

SCARLETT

"*Mommy*, who's gonna stay wif me?"

Tillie had asked me that exact question at least ten times in the last hour. My answer was the same as it was the first time: I don't know.

"I hope it's Auntie Brie." She jumped up and down on her bed, and while she knew better, I loved seeing her carefree so I let it slide. I was right next to her so she wouldn't get hurt.

"We'll just have to wait and see." As the words left my mouth, the doorbell rang.

"They're here!" Tillie jumped one last time and landed on her butt to scoot off the bed. When her little feet hit the floor, she took off running.

"Tillie!" I called after her. "Don't answer that door without me."

The command didn't slow her down, but I easily caught up to her. She was laughing and clapping, her excitement unable to be contained. When I was a few feet from the door, Aiden's deep chuckle rumbled through the barrier, and I couldn't help but smile.

Tillie's hand was on the doorknob, and she looked at me expectantly.

"Go ahead."

I lowered my head to take in my outfit and smoothed my palms over my thighs. I hoped I looked okay. When I glanced back up, Aiden was staring, heat smoldering in his eyes. Tillie was in his arms, hers wrapped around his neck and she was trying to get his attention, but to no avail. His focus was locked on me. Heat crept into my cheeks, and tendrils of lust swirled at my core.

"Hi." I had to swallow several times to get the one-word greeting out.

"Wow." He shook his head, as if doing so would change the image before him. "You look incredible."

I wore jeans and a form-fitting periwinkle blue shirt with black angel wings emblazoned on the front. I also had on a pair of knee-high black leather boots. I hadn't asked but had silently hoped we'd be taking his bike wherever we were going.

"Thanks. You too." His cheeks grew ruddy at the compliment. "So, uh, babysitter?" I leaned sideways to see if I was missing something. He'd come into the house by himself and if he was alone, what did that mean for our date?

"Brie and Griff should be he—" Aiden whirled around at the sound of an engine. "Ah, there they are."

For a minute, I panicked. They were there to watch my four-year-old daughter and they brought a motorcycle? What were they thinking? What if something happened and they needed to take her to the hospital?

"Sugar, relax." My eyes shot to his as he stepped toward me with Tillie still on his hip.

"I am relaxed," I snapped.

"No, you're not. You've got that 'worried mama' look." He reached out and smoothed a fingertip across my forehead, presumably to smooth out the wrinkles. "We aren't going to be far, and Brie and Griffin will keep her safe. I promise. Besides, your car is here if they need it."

I blew out a breath and nodded. Tillie scrambled to be put down as her babysitters came up onto the porch. When her feet hit the ground, she ran to them and was scooped up and tossed in the air. Her giggles eased the tension coiled in my muscles as she was carried back into the house.

"Damn, Scarlett." Griffin whistled. "Aiden, man, I hope you've got a blanket to cover her up with, otherwise, you're gonna spend the evening fighting off other men." Aiden's eyes narrowed, and his fists clenched at his sides.

"Um, hello? Your wife is standing right here." Brie punched Griffin in the arm before crossing hers over her chest.

"Yes, she is." Griffin grinned before reaching out and tugging Brie toward him with the hand that wasn't holding Tillie. "And no one compares to you, baby. But I'm not dead."

"You're about to be," Aiden threatened, which only caused Griffin's grin to widen before Aiden turned his attention to Brie. "Control your man, before I have to."

"Nah, he's right." Brie turned to me. "You look great. Now, you two go have fun and we'll keep this little munchkin busy." She reached in and tickled Tillie.

"Thanks, guys. We really appreciate this." Aiden's tone was no longer threatening. He reached out and grabbed my hand, threading his fingers with mine. "You ready?"

"As I'll ever be." I leaned over to give Tillie a kiss on the cheek. "You be good." When Tillie nodded, I returned my focus to the adults. "My cell number's on the fri—"

"Sugar, they already have your number. And mine. Everything will be fine." He squeezed my hand in reassurance.

I drew in a few deep breaths before exhaling loudly. "Right. Okay."

Aiden tugged me toward the door, and before I could change my mind, he said, "We'll be back in a few hours. See ya later." And with that, he shut the door behind us.

He walked me down the steps and onto the sidewalk before coming to a halt in front of his bike. "This okay?"

I knew I shouldn't act too excited, encourage him in any way, but I couldn't help it. "It's perfect." I pulled out of his hold and threw a leg over the seat. He huffed out laughter at my excitement. "You coming?"

"Not yet, sugar." He shook his head. "Not yet." He stepped off the curb and straddled the bike in front of me before throwing a look over his shoulder. "Hold on tight."

I wrapped my arms around his waist and pressed my cheek against his back. It'd been a long time since I'd been on a bike. Roughly five years. I'd missed this, him. He was strong, solid... safe. He revved the engine and took off, heading down the street, slowly at first. After he'd wound his way through some of the side streets, he reached a back road and opened her up.

I leaned back a bit, wanting to feel the wind in my hair, on my face. Aiden's hand settled over mine and squeezed. I wanted to ask him where we were going, what his plan was, but he wouldn't have been able to hear me. He drove for another ten minutes or so before turning down a lane that I'd been down dozens of times.

We entered BRB property, but when we reached his house, he kept driving until he came to a gravel path I didn't recognize. When he came to a clearing, I could see a creek with a red and black checkered blanket spread out over the grass on the bank. There was a picnic basket as well, but that was it.

"Where are we?" I asked when we'd both gotten off the bike.

He didn't answer, but rather picked up my hand and

walked me to the blanket. He lowered himself down and opened the basket of food. I stared at him, torn between wanting an answer to my question and not giving a damn. Once he was satisfied that everything was laid out just the way he wanted it, he tilted his head back to look at me and smiled.

"You gonna stand there all night or sit down?"

I tucked my legs under me and sat but not without rolling my eyes at him. Fortunately, my boots didn't have a zipper because otherwise I wouldn't have been able to sit like that for long.

"Where are we?" I asked him again. It may have seemed trivial to him, especially since we'd clearly been on, or very near, his property, but for someone who'd spent the last four years running and hiding, not knowing where I was caused physical pain.

"Relax. We're still on BRB property." The corner of his mouth lifted. "Completely surrounded by security cameras and the best technology money can buy." He reached out and brushed my hair out of my face. "You're safe."

My shoulders rose and fell with my breath and I nodded. Rather than speak, Aiden handed me a sandwich, turkey breast and honey ham, and a bag of chips. I laughed at the simplicity of it, but secretly, I was thrilled that he had kept the meal minimal. Less pressure that way.

Aiden watched me eat with a look of wonder on his face. It unnerved me, but it also felt... good. Like he couldn't see enough of me. While he looked his fill, so did I. My gaze got hung up on the lines of his throat every time he swallowed. His hands were large holding the sandwich, but the bread didn't squish. I imagined those hands on my body, teasing my skin with their strength while also being gentle, purposeful.

When the food was gone, I couldn't tear my eyes away. He

cleared his throat, and my head rose so quickly the rushing blood made me a little dizzy.

"I brought you here for a date, not to have you undress me without any of the satisfaction." His eyes twinkled, but his muscles bunched. He was bothered by my obvious inspection, but lucky for him, his words were the ice water needed to cool me down.

"Hate to break it to you, but I haven't been on a date in… a long time. Besides, I seem to recall you enjoying the way I look at you."

"Sugar, I love the way you look at me, and I'm not telling you to stop. But I want you to see that there's more to us than sex. And if you keep eating me with your eyes, we're gonna have sex." His matter-of-fact tone was not lost on me.

"Aiden, sex with you is great. And I never said we couldn't have sex." His eyebrows rose to his hairline at that bit of information. I chuckled but continued. "But if you want something long term from me then there needs to be… more. And I'm just not sure we have the *more*."

"We do," he said simply. Those two words held more conviction than anything else he'd ever said to me. And I wanted to believe him. I really did. But he'd have to prove it to me.

You have to let him in a little if he's going to prove anything to you.

"Look, let's just enjoy the rest of the evening. Take things one day, one hour at a time. You said you'd give it, *us* a chance."

"You're right. I did." I tipped my head toward what remained of our picnic. "Good food, great location. What's next?"

"I'm not sure." He scratched his head as if he could dig the answer out of his brain. "I haven't exactly *dated* either." He got a sheepish look on his face and shrugged. "Can we just talk?"

"I've told you everything you want to know." I sighed, frustrated at his insistence that I keep reliving the bad.

"You haven't, but that's not what I meant. You said we need more than just sex so talking seems like a natural place to start." He held a finger to my lips to silence my protest. "I'm not asking you for more information about... things. I'm asking you about you."

"And what about you?" I asked when he lowered his finger. "I'm not the only one with a past. With secrets."

His eyes narrowed as he leaned back on his elbows. "What do you want to know?"

I shrugged. "Whatever you want me to know."

He stood and began to pace, beating the grass down with his boots. He shoved a frustrated hand through his hair several times. I'd given up on getting him to open up about anything when he sat back down and pulled me toward him, my back to his front. If he couldn't look at me while he talked then it must be bad.

"I didn't exactly have the same childhood you had." His heart was hammering so hard I could feel it against my spine. "My mother was young when she had me. She'd worked as a nanny for a prominent family. Apparently, the guy wasn't satisfied with his wife so he seduced my mother, knocked her up. When she found out, she'd planned to tell him but his wife somehow figured things out and paid her to leave and not say anything. So she did." His chin rested on my head. "In case you're wondering, I was valued at five grand."

His arms came around me and his hold tightened, almost painfully, but I didn't have the heart to say anything. I rested my hand on his forearm to offer comfort and after several seconds, some of the tension eased.

"Anyway, she blew through the money pretty fast and by

the time I was two, she'd started sleeping with whoever would have her, for a price. Eventually that price was drugs and she died of an overdose when I was six."

I wanted to tell him I was sorry, that he was just a kid and that should never have happened, but it wasn't enough. Nothing would be enough to erase that from a person's memory. Instead of saying anything, I managed to turn around in his hold and wrap my legs around his waist and my arms around his neck. I rested my head on his shoulder and whispered for him to continue.

"None of my mother's family wanted me. I was a bastard to them. So my father was called. The father who knew nothing about me."

At his words, I reared back and my hand came to my mouth. "That's why you were so angry with me."

He nodded. "It's more than that, though. I may have his DNA in me, but I'm nothing like him. I'm no saint, but I'd never cheat. I'd never be just a sperm donor." He looked at me with a hint of anger. "Not on purpose, at least."

I hung my head in shame. His words hurt but only because they were true. My actions made him a sperm donor. I'd made choices that put him in a position he never would have willingly been in. His hand came under my chin and forced me to look at him.

"I'm not telling you this to make you feel guilty. I'm telling you this because you need to understand who I am. As a person. As a man. Who I'll be as a partner, a father." He dropped his hand and looked past me, staring at nothing but seeming to see everything. "My father refused to take me in. He denied his affair with my mother, and his wife never admitted what she'd done. So I bounced around from one foster home to another. Some were worse than others, but all of them were hell."

"Did your father ever reach out? Acknowledge you?"

He shook his head. "When I turned eighteen, I tried to track him down. I was determined to prove to him who I was. That I was his. I'd worked odd jobs during high school and saved up all of my money. I hired a private investigator. Fortunately, he found my father quickly because he was fucking expensive."

"How did it go when you saw him? Your father?" My gut clenched as I waited for the answer.

"It didn't." He finally looked at me, and his eyes were shimmering. I didn't know if he was tearing up because he was sad or angry but either way, I wanted to make it better. "He'd died. Had a heart attack not long after he refused to take me in. I told myself that the guilt was too much for him, but the fact of the matter is, it didn't change anything. It didn't make what he did any less wrong. It wasn't justice or karma or whatever you want to call it. It just… was."

"What did you do after that?"

"Joined the Navy. Put all of that pent-up pain and anger into serving my country. I was damn good too." He grinned and that's when I knew that his past hadn't broken him. It may have shaped who he was and how he viewed the world, but it didn't define him.

Why are you letting yours define you?

That was a good question. Aiden offered me a chance to do just that. Move on. Live a happy life.

What about Justin?

Another good question. I couldn't move on, be happy, with Justin still out there somewhere. It wasn't fair to Aiden or anyone else for that matter.

"What are you thinking about?" Aiden's voice broke through my thoughts.

"Nothing."

"Bullshit. Don't lie to me, Scarlett. Not ever. You did that once and look where it got you."

I reeled from his words as if he'd physically slapped me across the face, and anger flowed through my veins.

"I did what I had to!"

"You keep saying that." He reached out, and I dodged his touch. "Who are you trying to convince? Me or you?"

My breath whooshed out of me as I contemplated his question. I'd made the choices I made because, at the time, I thought it had been the right thing to do. I hadn't known Aiden well enough to have a baby with him, and despite everything Justin seemed like the safer road. I'd been wrong on so many levels.

"Fine. Maybe it wasn't the right thing to do. But I can't go back and change things."

"No, you can't. No one can. But don't make the same mistake twice."

"What are you talking about?"

"Me." His tone became pleading. "We get a second chance. Not many people can say that. C'mon, Scarlett. I'm here for a reason. You reached out to me for a reason. Let me in."

I chewed on my bottom lip, and he reached out and traced a line down my cheek. His features softened, and his eyes focused on my mouth. His pupils dilated, and he leaned forward and touched his lips to mine.

He didn't linger, didn't press for more. When he sat back, I wanted to follow his body, meld mine to his and never let them part. Instead, I pushed to my feet and walked down the bank to the creek. He followed and his hand rested at the small of my back.

"Let me in, Scarlett. I'm not going to hurt you."

"I'm not worried about me." I turned around to face him. "You don't get it. Sure, I left because I thought it was what was best for me, for Tillie. But I stayed away because I thought it was what was best for you."

20

AIDEN

Best for me.

Those words swirled around in my head like the last of the Rice Krispies in a bowl of milk. After Scarlett made that confession, I'd changed the subject. Not because I didn't want to hear more but because I'd never intended for our date to turn into rehashing what went down between us. I wanted to know what she'd been thinking, of course, but like she said, it didn't change anything.

"I had a good time tonight." I turned around on the seat of Calypso so I could face her. We were parked in her driveway, and I knew that we were likely being watched by Brie and Griffin from the window, but I didn't care.

"Me too." Her lashes lowered for a split second before she pierced me with her luminous eyes. A tear snaked down her cheek, and I brushed it away with the pad of my thumb.

"Why the tears?"

She swiped at her cheek and sniffled. "I really screwed up, didn't I?"

"Ah, not so much." When she looked at me like she didn't

believe me, I chuckled. "Sugar, when you love someone, that means you love every part of them. No matter what."

"But…"

"But nothing. I love you. I will always love you. You can put me through whatever test you want, make me wait a month, try to convince me that it's a bad idea, but that will never change."

"How do you know?"

"Because you walked away before, and I was still here for you to come back to. Because you gave birth to my daughter, without me, and I was still here for you to come back to." I took a deep breath. "Because I tried like hell to get over you, and I was still here for you to come back to."

"So what now?"

"Now?" My shoulders rose and fell. "I continue to woo you while we sort out this mess with your ex."

"You make it sound so easy." She grabbed my hand and gripped it tight, letting some of her fear become apparent. "But it's not."

"Nothing worthwhile is ever easy, sugar."

"You guys gonna sit out there all night or what?" Griffin's voice boomed through the night air. "I'd like to get my wife home and—"

"We don't need details, man." I rolled my neck before swinging my leg over the seat and helping Scarlett to stand. "Sorry 'bout that. He's an ass."

"You still love him, though." Her smile betrayed the confusion in her eyes.

"Damn straight." I walked her toward the porch, my arm slung over her shoulders. "He's always there, no matter what. He'd die for me and I for him. Doesn't mean he doesn't piss me the fuck off sometimes."

She stopped walking, forcing me to stop with her. She

turned to face me, and her eyes were huge, indecision pooling in them.

"Do you, uh…"

"Do I what, sugar?" I cupped her cheek and she leaned into my touch.

"I can't think when you do that."

I didn't stop.

"Do you wanna stay tonight? I mean, you don't have to if you—"

"Yes. I wanna."

∽

The moment we walked in the door, Scarlett had tensed up, like she'd been second-guessing her decision to ask me to stay. I had no doubts about being exactly where I was meant to be, but I didn't push her.

Tillie was sound asleep in her bed. Griffin and Brie had left. We'd been alone for an hour and had done nothing more than talk. About everything from movies to television to food to the weather. Basically anything other than about us, love, family. Throughout the entire conversation, there'd been flirty looks and careful touches. I'd wanted to ravage her, but I'd held back, for her sake.

"Want another beer?" Scarlett stood to return to the kitchen.

I tracked her movement, my cock jumping at the sway of her hips. She was still in her skintight jeans but gone were the boots. It'd be a pleasure to slide the denim down her legs, baring her to me. What material would I find covering her pu—

"Aiden?" My head whipped up at the sound of her voice. She was back in front of me, a beer thrust in my direction.

"Uh, thanks." I took a swig and let the liquid coat my

throat and prayed that it would calm my lust. It didn't. "So, uh, wanna watch a movie?"

"Not really." Her lashes briefly lowered as she placed one knee on the couch next to me and then the other. "Do you?"

"I thought…"

"Stop thinking." Her hand came up, and her fingers threaded in my short hair. Her touch electrified me.

"Sugar, are you sure you want to open that can of worms?"

Rather than speak, she nodded before locking her lips with mine. Hers were warm, plump, and I could taste the alcohol she'd consumed along with a hint of her peach lip gloss. I wrapped my arms around her and slid them down the back of her jeans to cup her ass and pull her closer. She had yet to open her mouth to me, so I teased her lips with my tongue, urging her to open up.

When our tongues collided, a growl filled the room and I realized it was my own. Heat surged through my veins, and I thought I was going to combust. Scarlett's hands went from my hair to my chest. She pressed her body firmly against mine, and I pulled back to stare into her eyes.

"This is your last chance to back out, sugar." I'd stop if she asked me to, but it'd be fucking difficult.

"I just want to feel something good. Remind me of how good it can be."

That was all I needed to hear. I stood, lifting her with me and her legs wrapped around my waist. As I carried her up the stairs our mouths crashed and our tongues teased, tempted. I kicked her door open and winced at the sound. I'd momentarily forgotten that Tilllie was asleep just down the hall. That would take some getting used to.

When I reached the bed and bent to lay Scarlett down, she tried to pull me with her, but I managed to extricate myself. Her eyes bore into mine but only until I started to strip. That's when she sat up and her gaze wavered, traveled from my face down to my toes, stopping to hungrily stare at my junk.

She reached down to pull her top over her head, but I lunged forward and grabbed her hands to halt her progress. I placed my hands on her shoulders and guided her back down onto the bed before straddling her hips and caging her in.

"Naked, Aiden. I want to be naked," she pleaded.

"We'll get there, sugar." I slid her shirt up to just under her breasts and trailed a circle around her belly button. She shivered and moaned. "Are you going to be able to be quiet?"

"I've never been quiet with you." She quickly glanced at the door and sighed, as if just remembering that there was a child not too far from us. "But I'll do my best."

"Good girl."

I leaned down and replaced my fingertips with my tongue while I unbuttoned her jeans and lowered the zipper. A scrap of pale blue fabric peaked out from between the flaps, and my mouth went dry. Bone dry.

I knew I should go slow, take my time and enjoy every last second, but being so close to my target amped up my need. I tapped Scarlett's thigh the way I used to, and she lifted her hips so I could tear her jeans and panties off. I slid back up her body and rid her of her shirt and lace bra, baring all of her flesh to me. I sat back on my haunches and memorized every fuckable inch.

Whimpers escaped her as I looked my fill, telling me she wanted more than just my scrutiny. I covered her body with mine, letting my cock rub against her. Every point of contact was like a bolt of lightning. I pressed a kiss to the jumping pulse point at her throat. Her nails raked down my back, the pain a welcome sensation as it morphed into something more, something better.

"I'm going to make you wish you could scream," I whispered in her ear right before nipping at the lobe and sucking it into my mouth.

I sat up and made my way down her torso, leaving a trail of goosebumps with my tongue. I detoured to devour her hip bone and reached my hands up to tweak her nipples which were tight buds of need. When I was done teasing her I veered toward the spot that I craved more than my next breath.

"Oh god, sweet Jesus, oh…" she panted the second the tip of my tongue touched and curled around her clit.

I hummed against her, and she bucked against the vibration. I brought an arm down and rested it on her stomach to anchor her in place. My other hand joined my mouth, one finger crooking inside her, then another.

The tell-tale clenching began slowly so I increased the speed of my tongue and pressure of my fingers. Scarlett let out a deep moan, and the next thing I knew, she thrust her hips off the bed and dug her heels in. I didn't let up until she floated back down and her wild shaking became sweet quivers.

"That was—"

"Incredible." I slid up her body and punctuated the word with a kiss. "Amazing." Kiss. "Intoxicating." Kiss. "Just the beginning."

Scarlett arched a brow and I grinned. She spread her legs as far as she could, opening herself to me before reaching down between our bodies and fisting my thick length. She squeezed and teased the tip with the pad of her thumb, swirling the pre-cum around and making me crazy. I would have exploded in her hand had she not let go to grab my hips and jerk me to her, impaling herself on my cock.

I stilled, wanting to savor the moment. Her eyes registered her pleasure, her desire matched my own.

"Ya gonna move?"

I bent and drew a nipple into my mouth. She squirmed at the sensation, and I slid out of her until my tip almost withdrew completely and then thrust back in. I maintained a slow pace until every muscle in my body strained to go faster, harder. I let my instincts take over and she matched my every thrust.

Scarlett tightened around me, and when her moans grew louder, I covered her mouth with my hand to keep her quiet. She shook uncontrollably, but I didn't slow down. My hips flew and when she was no longer bucking her hips to meet mine, my balls drew tight and I growled out my release.

I collapsed on top of her, and when I was able to move again, I rolled to the side, taking her with me. She curled into me, and I wrapped my arms around her, neither of us caring that there'd be a wet spot.

"We're gonna do that again, right?" Her muffled question reached my ears, and I huffed out a laugh. While I may not have been with her for the sex, there was no denying that it was fucking phenomenal.

"Sugar, we can do that as many times as you want, for as long as you want." I kissed the top of her head and she sighed.

We lay there, sated, silent, no sound other than my pounding heart and her breathing. When she relaxed in my hold, I knew she'd fallen asleep. I stared over her shoulder at the wall for a long time, wondering how I'd gotten so lucky.

It was that thought that took me into the deepest sleep I'd had in four years.

21

SCARLETT

"Make it stop."

Someone's cell phone beeped incessantly. It couldn't be mine. No one other than the BRB had the number. The events of last night slammed into me, and I realized it must be Aiden's phone. I reached out to smack him so he'd answer the damn thing, but my arm connected with fluffy blankets instead of hard muscle.

I sat up quickly and twisted to see the clock on the nightstand. It was only five, which explained why I didn't hear the ever present noises from Tillie. What it didn't explain was why I was alone in the bed. I pressed the palms of my hands to my eyes and rubbed the sleep from them.

There was still a beeping sound, and since Aiden wasn't there, it was likely my phone. I threw the covers back and swung my legs over the edge of the bed. I snatched my cell and glanced at the screen. My lungs seized, and my heart plummeted to my feet. There were notifications of texts, dozens of them, from an unknown number.

Unknown: Hi

Unknown: What are you doing?

Unknown: I miss you

Unknown: Hello?

Unknown: Don't you miss me?

They went on and on. None of them were threatening, and if I hadn't been on the run for so long I might have thought it was just a wrong number, but I had been, so it didn't seem likely.

I rushed to the door and ran down the hall to Tillie's room. I forced myself to slow down and open her door quietly. She was still sound asleep, her little body peaceful and relaxed. I breathed a sigh of relief that whatever this was hadn't reached her... yet.

I glanced down at the device in my hand and chewed on the inside of my cheek. I should call Aiden, let him see the messages and determine if it was something I should worry about. But no. He'd left. Snuck away in the middle of the night like what we'd done should somehow be kept a secret. A dirty secret.

Anger at his actions surged through my veins, and I left the room so I could unleash my wrath without Tillie waking up. I stomped down the steps to the living room and dialed his number. While it rang, I paced. Aiden's voicemail picked up just as the front door swung open.

I whirled around at the sound and there he stood, his arms filled with bags. He held them up and grinned like a cat proudly bringing its master its dead mouse bounty. I stood there, mouth and eyes wide, several questions swirling around in my mind. I asked the one that seemed the most pressing, based on the fear from the texts.

"How'd you get in?"

He tilted his head, as if trying to place the emotion in my voice. "I have a key, remember?"

"Oh, right." I shoved my hands through my hair and scrubbed them down my face. "I forgot."

"You forgot?" He walked to the kitchen to deposit the bags on the island and then returned and pulled me toward him. "I can buy that you forgot, but what I don't get is why you looked about ready to clobber me when I walked in."

I let my head rest against his chest and breathed in his scent. He was dressed in the same clothes he'd had on the night before, but he still smelled incredibly good.

"You left."

He tugged my hair to get me to look up at him. There were creases on his forehead, and he wore a frown. "I didn't *leave*. I thought I'd make you and Tillie pancakes for breakfast, and you didn't have what I needed. I ran to the store." He stroked my hair. "And came back."

He had come back, so why couldn't I shake the feeling of dread settling in my stomach? My eyes slid closed and I focused on the feel of his body pressed against mine. His lips touched mine in a feather light kiss. When he pulled back, he stepped away and grabbed my hand to tug me to the couch. We both sat and he stared at me like he was trying to figure something out.

"Sugar, what aren't you saying?"

I shook my head. "Nothing."

He sighed and leaned back against the arm of the sofa. He glanced down at my hand, the one that still gripped my cell. I followed his line of sight and realized that my knuckles were white from clenching so tightly. He returned his focus to me and cocked an eyebrow.

"What?" I snapped, knowing I needed to tell him about the texts and at the same time, not wanting to.

"You tell me," he said patiently.

We sat there, in silence, for what felt like hours but was only minutes. Aiden waited me out, knowing that I'd give in and tell him what he wanted to know but also not pushing me.

"When I woke up, I thought I was hearing your phone go off. But it was mine." I lifted the phone, tapped the screen to wake it up and turned it to show him the messages.

He took the cell from me and scrolled through them, his eyes narrowing and his jaw hardening. When he was done, he took his own phone out of his pocket, hit a button and then held the phone face up in front of him. I could tell he was making a call and the screen read 'Griff'. He'd put it on speaker phone.

"What're you—"

"This had better be important." My question went unfinished because Griffin answered on the fourth ring and sounded pissed.

"Of course it's important."

"Give me a sec." The sound of rustling came through the line, and I realized that Aiden's call had woken Griffin up. There was another voice in the background, demanding that Griffin 'come back to bed', but it faded and disappeared right after the sound of a door closing registered. "Okay. Go."

"Get to your computer. I need you to check a few things."

"You're a demanding asshole, you know that?"

"Just do it."

"Can I at least make some coff—"

"No." Aiden was doing his best not to shout, but he was fast losing patience with Griffin. "Computer. Now." He sighed and reached out to touch my leg as if anchoring himself in place. "Please."

"Well, since you asked so nicely." There was humor in Griffin's tone, mixed with residual frustration. "While everything is booting up, fill me in. What exactly are you needing me to do?"

"I need you to get into Scarlett's phone. It should already be linked to your software." Aiden held up his hand when I started to protest. "I need you to pull up her text messages."

"Okay." The word was drawn out, and the next thing I heard was what sounded like fingers flying over a keyboard. "I'm in. I take it your phone call has something to do with all of the ones from the unknown number?"

"You're a genius." Sarcasm dripped from Aiden's tone. "Can you trace those back to anyone?"

"Does a bear shit in the woods? Of course I can trace it."

"Call me when you've got something."

"You got—"

Aiden hit the 'end' button, and the phone went silent.

I clenched my fists in my lap. Not only were the texts disturbing, but now I had to worry about all of my communication being monitored by the BRB. I knew that they'd put some things in place for security reasons, but I'd never imagined this.

"You hungry?" He stood and started to walk to the kitchen.

"Are you fucking serious right now?" I rose and followed.

"If you're not hungry, all you gotta do is say so." He didn't turn around and look at me when he spoke but rather, he rummaged through the cabinets until he found what he was looking for.

He put a pan on the stove, turned the burner on and got the pancake ingredients out of one of the bags he'd brought in earlier. He started to make breakfast, and I stood there, staring, unable to comprehend that he wasn't picking up my frustration.

"Aiden, stop!"

I grabbed his arm and tried to spin him around to face

me, but he didn't budge. He did tense up, his spine stiffening and his muscles bunching under his shirt. He glanced at my hand, and I yanked it back as if burned.

He twisted the knob to turn the stove back off and slowly turned to face me with his arms crossed over his chest.

"Look, you're pissed. I get that. But I won't apologize. Not for doing whatever is necessary to keep you and Tillie safe."

"And bugging my phone does that?"

"I didn't bug your phone. Jesus, I'm not a creep." His arms dropped to his sides. "But yes, there is software on there that will help trace calls and texts. And apparently that was the right thing to do."

His face took on a smug look, and I wanted to smack it off of him but I didn't. Once again, he was right but I hated that he hadn't told me about the software.

"Whatever. Just please don't keep things from me." Pretty hypocritical of me to want that, expect that, but I was beyond giving a damn.

"Scarlett, you have to trust me. I didn't intentionally keep anything from you. I just didn't think to tell you about every single precaution we took. I'm sor—"

Aiden's phone rang and he walked to the living room to answer it. He didn't put it on speaker phone this time, so I couldn't hear the entire conversation but what I did hear had me on edge.

"You're sure? No, I guess that's good, but it doesn't feel right. Yeah, I know but… Griff, there's no room for error on this one. Alright, alright. Yeah, great. I'll calm down when this fucking dick is behind bars or dead, whichever comes first. Fine. Okay, I'll let her know. Thanks."

Aiden ended the call, and when he turned he ran into me almost knocking me over. He'd been so absorbed in his call that he hadn't heard me walk up behind him. He reached out to steady me, and his touch set me on fire.

"Turns out we worried for nothing." The words were right, but the look on his face said something else entirely.

"You don't look convinced. And you sure as hell didn't sound convinced on the phone."

"Griffin's the best, and he has yet to get bad intel but…"

"But what?"

"He traced the call back to some kid. A dig into social media showed that it was a girl who'd recently been dumped. Her ex's phone number is one digit different than yours, and she must have made a mistake." His shoulders slumped.

"Okay. This is good news." I reached out and rested my hand on his forearm. "So why can't you just accept it for what it is?"

"This is too damn important, that's why. You aren't just some client." He started to pace, his shoes thudding on the hardwood floor. "Any other client and I wouldn't sweat it. I'd take the information and be happy." He stopped and his eyes bore into mine with a look of anguish. "But this is different. You're different."

I reached up and cupped his cheek. He covered my hand with his and leaned into my touch. "If Griffin says it's nothing, then it's nothing. You taught me that. To trust the BRB with my life. And I do. Why can't you?"

"You still don't get it, do you?"

"Get what?"

"That I love you. That if anything happened to you, or to Tillie, I'd never forgive myself. I've broken every boundary that I'd ever set for myself. And I wouldn't unbreak them even if I could. I can't treat you like everyone else. I won't."

"I'm not asking you to. But I am asking you to not freak out when there's nothing to freak out about. Griffin checked the texts out. They're nothing. An honest mistake. Let it go."

"Fine." He didn't look like he was going to let it go, but I chose to move the conversation in a different direction. Distract him.

"I'm getting hungry. How 'bout I go wake up Tillie and we have breakfast? Sound good?"

It took him a few seconds to shake off whatever it was he had going on in that head of his.

"Sounds great." He smiled but it didn't reach his eyes.

While he made pancakes, I woke Tillie up and got her ready for the day. We all ate breakfast, as a family, at the table, and it felt good. Right. Once the dishes were cleaned and put away, Aiden said he had some things to do but that he would call me later. That was good because I wanted to do some shopping. After he left, I got a quick shower while Tillie watched cartoons.

When it was time to leave, I opened the door, and Tillie and I stepped out onto the porch. I turned to face the barrier so I could lock up but felt Tillie pull on my shirt. I looked down at her, and she was pointing to her left. I followed her finger and smiled.

On one of the Adirondack chairs that Aiden bought me was a bouquet of red roses. I pulled my key from the lock and slipped the keychain over my wrist. I picked up the flowers and brought them up to my face to take a whiff. When I did, my nose bumped a card, and it drifted to the wooden planks. Tillie was next to me in an instant, picking the card up and handing it to me.

I took it and slipped it out of the miniature envelope, my heartbeat racing at what it would say. 'I love you', perhaps? When I unfolded the paper and read the words, the flowers fell from my hands and landed with a quiet thud.

YOU THOUGHT THEY WERE FROM *HIM*, DIDN'T YOU?

22

AIDEN

It'd been three days since Scarlett had gotten those text messages. I hadn't been able to see her because I'd been helping out with a new case, but we'd talked, texted. She'd told me that she'd enrolled Tillie in Pre-school and that she'd gone to Dusty's to see about a job.

That would be good for her because Dusty knew what we did, the kind of people that the BRB helps, and he wouldn't worry about things like legal names, social security numbers, or anything else that could tie Scarlett to this place. She got the job and would be paid under the table. I hated that it was necessary, but until Justin was behind bars, or six feet under, she couldn't be too careful. Added bonus, I loved Dusty's bar so it wouldn't be a hardship to keep an eye on her. Not that it ever was.

While all of that was good, it had still been three days, and I needed to see her, touch her, kiss her. I was picking Tillie up from school while Scarlett worked, and she'd meet us at her place. I was thrilled to be spending time alone with my daughter but nervous too. Why, I had no idea. It wasn't like I hadn't been alone with her before, when Scarlett was in the hospital. But this was different.

I pulled the Jeep up to the small building that housed the pre-school and parked. There were numerous other cars parked on the little side street, and it occurred to me that the building wasn't on a main road which meant the security of it wasn't as good. It was an old building, brick exterior with two entrances, neither of which looked secure.

I walked inside, tension knotting my muscles as I realized that my assessment was spot on. No security. I made a mental note to talk to Scarlett about possibly switching Tillie to a different school. There were several in the county so it could be done easily.

"Aiden, what are you doing here?"

I turned toward the silky smooth voice, shocked that I was hearing it in this place, surrounded by children. The last time I'd heard it was the same day my life had taken a sharp turn. *What was her name?*

"Picking up my daughter."

Her face scrunched up but only for a second. I took a moment to assess her. She was in a black pantsuit with a red blouse and black pumps. She looked nothing like the woman I'd met at the bar and taken home to bury myself in. Nothing like the woman who'd cussed me out and thrown things at me as she'd stormed out of my house.

"You're married?" Her voice was accusatory, and I imagined if we were anywhere else she would have slung venom at me.

"No. Of course not." It pissed me off that she could think that, but I reminded myself that she knew nothing about me so it was a logical conclusion. "Look..." *Why couldn't I remember her name?*

"Lisa."

"Right, Lisa. We had a fun night, but clearly we don't

know each other. And that's not going to change. So, if you're done, I'd like to get my daughter."

"Wow. Just… wow." She glared at me before brushing past me into the throngs of kids.

I watched as she stopped next to a little boy with curly brown hair and a Spiderman T-shirt. She helped him put his jacket on as he talked non-stop and wiggled around making the task difficult. She never lost patience, though, which was completely out of character with the woman I'd known.

You didn't know her. You fucked her once.

I pushed my thoughts aside, as well as the disgust with myself, and looked around for Tillie. There were lots of children and adults picking them up, but no Tillie. My heart plummeted to my stomach, and my spine stiffened. I turned in circles, hoping that I was just missing her somehow, but nothing. I stormed over to one of the teachers, a short woman who appeared to be in her late thirties and who had nailed the school marm look.

"Where's my daughter?"

"And who's your daughter?" She peered up at me from behind her thick framed glasses before inching them up her nose with a fingertip.

"Tillie. Tillie Runyon." We really needed to do something about that last name. It should be Winters. "She just started yesterday."

"Ah, yes. Tillie's a very sweet little girl." She turned away from me to survey the other kids in the room.

"She is. Now, where is she?" Each second we wasted discussing her personality was another second that she could be in danger.

"She was just here, so she couldn't have gotten far." She walked away from me and spoke to several of the other kids, as well as adults, presumably to see if anyone had seen Tillie. When she was done, she returned to my side. "Mr…"

"Winters. Aiden Winters. Where the he—"

A tug on my shirt had me whirling around and glancing down. Tillie stood there with a huge smile on her face, and all of the fear and worst case scenarios melted away. I bent down on one knee and smiled back at her.

"Hey peanut. We were looking for you."

"I hadda go to the bathroom."

"Ah, okay." I looked over my shoulder at the teacher and she tilted her head as if curious about the interaction between father and daughter. Rather than let that bother me, I focused my attention back on Tillie. "Ready to head home?"

She nodded her head vigorously, her little blonde curls bouncing. She ran to get her backpack, a little blue number with what I'd learned was Elsa from *Frozen* on it. I helped her put her arms through the straps and held her hand as we walked outside. Several of the other kids waved 'goodbye' to Tillie, and she did the same. It was good to see her making friends. I imagined she hadn't been able to do much of that before.

On the drive to Scarlett's house, Tillie chattered about her day, but as we got closer, she got quiet. I glanced in the rearview mirror and noted that she had fallen asleep. Apparently, pre-school was exhausting.

When we pulled into the driveway, I noticed that there was a box on the porch and wondered what Scarlett had ordered. I'd have to talk to her about buying things online. Stuff like that could be traced.

"Peanut, we're home."

I turned in my seat and gently shook her leg to wake her up. I could've just carried her inside but knew that if she slept too long, it would be hell getting her to bed later. Tillie stirred and rubbed her fists over her eyes.

"Ready to go inside?"

She nodded so I got out and then lifted her out of her car

seat. When her feet hit solid ground, she took off running and stopped when she got to the door. I chuckled as I followed her, wishing I had half as much energy as she did.

I picked up the box and warning bells went off when I saw that there was no shipping label. What kind of online retailer doesn't use a shipping label? I glanced up and down the street to see if there was anything or anyone that seemed out of place. Nothing.

"Peanut, do you know if mommy was expecting anything?" The box was very light and I flipped it over several times, trying to figure out what it could be.

"I dunno." She shrugged but then her eyes lit up. "Maybe it's flowers like before."

My head snapped to her, and my gut clenched. "What do you mean?"

"Mommy got flowers. She said they was fwom a fwiend." As she spoke, she twisted the doorknob, but it was locked, so it didn't budge.

I shook my head, clearing my racing thoughts and focused on getting her inside. I helped her change into play clothes and then prepared her a little snack. She wanted to watch a movie, so I set her up in the living room while I stayed in the kitchen to inspect the mysterious package.

I took pictures of the box with my cell, although I was pretty sure they wouldn't be helpful. The box was your basic shipping box: brown cardboard. It hadn't been taped shut but rather the flaps had been folded in such a way that the box stayed closed.

I opened it and white-hot rage took over. Inside, nestled in bubble wrap, was a glass figurine of a long-stemmed red rose. I lifted it out and set it on the counter before pulling out all of the wrap, making sure there was nothing else. There was. Two photographs were at the bottom. One was of Scarlett and Tillie, and I could tell it was taken recently because they were standing on a sidewalk and in the background was an antique shop in town. As if that wasn't bad enough, both faces had a red 'X' over them.

The second picture was even more shocking. It was of me, although it wasn't quite as recent. I was standing in front of the hospital and based on the look on my face, it was taken the day I got the call about Scarlett. My face also had a red 'X' over it.

I put everything back in the box so Tillie wouldn't see it and glanced toward the living room to make sure she was still settled on the couch. Satisfied that she was, I pulled my phone out of my pocket and called Griffin.

"He's here," I said when he answered.

"Who's where?"

"Justin. He's here, in town."

"What the fuck? How do you know?" Anger infused his voice. We'd all been working to find this guy, but we'd struck out.

"When I got to Scarlett's house after picking Tillie up from school, there was a package on the porch." I went on to describe the contents, Griffin injecting muttered cuss words as I did. "And Tillie said that there were flowers the other day."

"I take it Scarlett hadn't filled you in on that?"

"Hell no, she didn't," I snapped. I looked toward the living room to make sure my outburst hadn't disturbed Tillie. It hadn't. I lowered my voice. "If she had, I'd be hunting this dick down, not standing in her kitchen while Tillie watches Frozen for the thousandth time."

"Calm down, man. You don't want to scare her."

I shoved a stiff hand through my hair. He was right, but it was damn hard to remain calm.

"I took pictures of everything. I'll text them to you, although I'm not sure if there are any clues as to where he is."

"Send 'em over. I'll call Micah and we'll start working on our end." He sighed. "Don't go too hard on Scarlett when she gets home. She's used to dealing with this shit on her own. It's going to take her some time to bring you in on it."

"She already fucking brought me in on it," I said as my fist came down on the granite countertop. I clenched my teeth against the pain that radiated from my wrist to my elbow. "But I hear ya."

"Do you want me to send Brie over? Sadie? Maybe they could help when Scarlett gets home. With Tillie?"

"No, they can't do anything I can't, where Scarlett's concerned. And as far as Tillie goes, man we're a family. We're going to have to learn how to do things together and with her around. We can't always just shove her off on someone else."

"True. Okay, I'll get started. Head straight to our place when you get back."

"Got it. And Griffin?" I paused. "Thanks. I appreciate it."

"No thanks necessary. It's what we do. Besides, we're family. I'm not doing anything you haven't already done for me."

My throat closed up, and for a moment, I thought I'd lose it. I nodded but then realized that he couldn't see me. "Right."

"Send those pics and then go hang out with your daughter until Scarlett gets home. We got this." With that, he disconnected the call.

I stared at my phone for a minute before going to the photo app and selecting the ones that I needed to send to him. Text sent, I shoved my phone back into my pocket as I glanced at the package and decided to take Griff's advice.

I spent the next two hours on the couch, pretending that I wasn't seething inside and dying to tear someone apart.

"I'm home."

Scarlett sounded cheerful as she walked through the door. Tillie jumped up and ran to her, throwing her arms around her legs.

"Hey baby." Scarlett knelt down and smiled. "How was school?"

Tillie spent the next few minutes recounting everything she'd already told me. Scarlett listened, much like I had. The only difference being that it was obvious that their bond was deeper, stronger, than mine was with Tillie.

Give it time. Yours will be that deep, that strong.

"Hey, peanut. Why don't you go to your room while Mommy and I talk?"

Scarlett gave me a quizzical look, but Tillie didn't think twice about it. She ran up the steps and pretty soon the sounds of her playing with her toys drifted down the staircase to us.

"Thanks for picking her up." Scarlett walked to the couch and threw her purse down. She took her coat off and tossed it over the back of the sofa.

I stepped up behind her and wrapped my arms around her waist. "You don't have to thank me." I nuzzled her neck, and she tipped her head to the side, granting me better access.

"Was there something we needed to talk about?" Her voice was barely above a whisper.

"In a minute."

I nipped at her ear and then turned her around and pressed my straining erection into her belly. It was crazy how I could go from incredible rage and worry to horny as hell in a matter of seconds around her.

Scarlett's arms went around my neck, and she raised herself up on tiptoes to fuse her lips with mine. When her tongue teased mine, the package was momentarily forgotten

I found the hem of her shirt with my fingertips and skimmed them under and up to her full breasts. She arched her back and pressed herself into me. I kneaded her through the lace of her bra and then tugged the cups down and felt the weight of her in my hands.

Her nipples pebbled under my touch, and my cock grew harder. I briefly thought about stripping her naked, bending her over the couch and slamming into her from behind. I didn't though. Sanity crept back in, and I willed myself to stop. I broke the kiss and stepped back, dropping my hands to my sides. Her eyes flew open, and the blue appeared to pulsate around her pupils.

"Why'd you stop?"

"Sugar, if I didn't, we could've given Tillie quite a show. Not really interested in scarring her for life."

She chuckled. "Good point."

"Besides, we need to talk." I stepped around her and retrieved the package from the kitchen counter.

She followed me and when I turned around to face her, box in hand, her face paled.

"What's that?"

"It was on the porch when we got home." I took a step toward her and she took a step back, away from me.

"But what is it?" Her fists were clenched at her sides, the knuckles white. She was still pale and looked scared to death.

"I'm guessing a follow-up to the flowers you got the other day." I quirked an eyebrow, and although I didn't think it possible, she grew paler.

"How did you know about those?" Her hand went to her throat, then she wrapped it around the back of her neck.

"I think the more important question is why did you keep it from me?"

Her shoulders slumped, and her hand dropped to her side. She was looking at me, but there was something about her eyes that told me she wasn't really seeing me. I took another step toward her and realized I was right when she didn't retreat or resist my touch when I cupped her cheek with my free hand.

"Sugar, look at me."

"I am."

"No, you're looking through me. I need you to look *at* me."

It took a minute, but her eyes focused. A suspicious sheen formed, and the next thing I knew, a tear was zigzagging down her cheek. I brushed it away with my thumb before moving my hand to the back of her head and pulling her to my chest.

"Why didn't you tell me?" I asked again, needing an answer.

"I don't know. I guess part of me was hoping it was just a fluke, that I was worrying for nothing." Her voice was muffled by my T-shirt, but I heard the resignation in it.

"It doesn't matter if it's a fluke or not. I need to know everything." I rubbed circles over her back, and when she tried to pull away, I held on tighter. She wasn't getting away from me that easy, or out of this conversation.

"Aiden, you don't get it. I've finally started to reclaim myself, who I am without all the crazy. I couldn't bear the thought I'd have to give it all up."

"You don't have to give anything up. You hear me? Nothing."

When she pulled away this time, I let her but kept my hand on her arm. She looked me in the eye and smiled.

"You're too good to be true."

"Sugar, don't make that mistake again. You did once and it cost us both so much. We're in this together, but it only works out if we're both completely honest. No secrets."

She nodded and blew out a breath. "No secrets." She eyed

the box I was still holding wearily. "You gonna show me what's in that, or do I have to use my imagination?"

I hesitated, not wanting to upset her. *No secrets.* My conscience wouldn't allow me to forget what I'd only moments ago made her promise, so I turned to go back to the kitchen and set the package on the counter.

"Now don't go panicking on me. I've already got Griffin working on things. We'll get this sorted out." I glanced at her out of the corner of my eye. I had yet to take any of the contents out, wanting to protect her, shield her from the insanity of it all.

"Let's just get this over with," she huffed as she reached out and started taking the contents out and placing them on the counter. When the glass rose and photos were laid out before her, she didn't say a word, just stared.

"I know how this must make you feel bu—"

"You can't possibly know," she snapped. Her hands gripped the edge of the counter as if she needed it to stay upright. "Oh my God. This is why I stayed away so long. I had to protect you. I couldn't let this evil touch you." She whirled around and started to pace. "We gotta go. I can't stay here. I can pack and be outta—"

"Scarlett, stop," I demanded, gripping her arm and spinning her to face me. "You aren't going anywhere, unless it's to my house. You hear me?"

"I have to. Don't you see? He's doing it again. Only this time, he'll get you too." Tears streamed down her face, and I had to admit, I preferred her anger to this.

"Nobody is going to *get me*. That's not going to happen. And he won't get you or Tillie either." Panic welled inside of me. I had to get her to see that their safest option was me. I couldn't let them get away again. Not when I'd had a taste of life with them, as a family. "Promise me you won't leave. Promise me you'll let me protect you."

"No. No, no, no. This can't be happening. I have to stop it. Stop him."

She yanked out of my hold and bolted for the steps. I let her go. She was going upstairs, and if it was to pack, then I'd stop her before she set foot out of the house.

I plopped down on the couch and stood right back up. I had too much fury flowing through my veins to sit still.

I put everything back in the box and took it out to the Jeep. That could have waited until I left, but I was trying to occupy myself so that I didn't storm upstairs. I glanced at the clock and noticed that it was past dinnertime and knew that Tillie had to be getting hungry.

I grabbed what I needed out of the refrigerator and cupboards and started to make a simple supper of tomato soup and toasted cheese sandwiches. I didn't feel much like eating, but this wasn't about me. While I worked, I stayed alert in case Scarlett tried to flee out the front door when I was occupied.

Once everything was ready, I decided that she'd had enough time to stew, so I went upstairs. Scarlett's voice floated through the air, and I determined that she was in Tillie's room. When I stepped through the doorway, I froze.

Tillie was sitting on the bed, hugging a teddy bear to her chest and crying while Scarlett was throwing as many toys and clothes as she could into a suitcase.

23

SCARLETT

"What the hell are you doing?"

I whirled around at Aiden's question, the pajamas I'd been about to put in the suitcase dropping to the floor.

"What does it look like?" I turned away from his cold, angry stare and bent to pick up the fallen clothes.

Footsteps thudded on the hardwood floor, and the shirt and pants were yanked from my grasp and thrown back to the floor. Aiden's posture was ramrod straight, and the veins in his neck were pronounced. He was beyond pissed.

"So that's it? Things get a little scary and you give in?" He crossed his arms over his chest and widened his stance, giving off a dangerous vibe. "Sugar, I've got news for you. You're not leaving, and you sure as fuck ain't taking my daughter."

"You gotta put money in the swear jar."

I'd been so focused on Aiden and his rage that I'd forgotten Tillie was in the room. I glanced at her and, while she was still crying, her voice conveyed no fear, which surprised me considering the circumstances.

Aiden looked at her, and his expression softened. "You're right, peanut." He pulled out his wallet and handed her a twenty. "Hold on to this for me, okay?"

"'Kay," she said as she gripped the bill tightly.

"Mommy and Daddy are going to talk. How 'bout you play in here while we do?" Aiden gripped my hand and tugged me toward the door as he spoke.

"'Kay, Daddy."

Aiden stopped in his tracks and looked at Tillie with laser-like focus at the title. His eyes widened and became glassy. He dropped my hand and walked back to the bed to pick Tillie up and give her a hug. She wrapped her arms around his neck and squeezed.

"Love you, peanut." Aiden's voice was thick and barely above a whisper, but the words did something to me.

"Love you too."

I turned away from the sight of them, determined not to let it change my mind. We had to leave, for everyone's sake.

Do you though? Aiden can protect you.

He might be able to protect me, but what about himself? He didn't know the threat like I did. Justin wouldn't stop at tormenting me. He would do whatever it took to hurt the man who laid claim to what he thought was rightfully his: Tillie.

"Get out of your head." Aiden's whispered demand startled me.

I glanced over my shoulder at Tillie, and she was back on her bed but she was no longer crying. Instead, she was happily looking through a book and 'reading' to her teddy bear.

"C'mon. We need to talk."

I resisted Aiden's touch but trudged after him to my bedroom. He shut the door a little harder than necessary while I sat on the bed. When he stood in front of me, I could see that the anger had never left. He'd just masked it for Tillie's sake.

"What?" I snapped.

"You know damn well 'what'. You were going to leave."

"Still am." I stood and frustration slammed into me when I wasn't at eye level. Not that I ever was, but it sure would come in handy during an argument. Hard to take someone seriously when they're staring at your chest.

Aiden gripped my chin and forced my gaze up to his. His eyes were hard, flinty orbs of rage. His jaw was clenched, and he was breathing through his nose, almost as if employing a deep breathing technique to calm down. We stared each other down for what felt like forever but was probably only seconds.

He relaxed his grip and the corners of his mouth rose into a mocking grin.

"Ain't happenin', sugar."

"Yeah, Aiden, it is." I blew out a breath. "I already called my dad, and he's booking us a flight."

As if on cue, my phone rang, and I glanced at the screen before answering. Unfortunately, I took a second too long because Aiden snatched the phone from my hand and answered it himself.

"Sir, this is Aiden Winters. Yes, she's safe, sir. No, I'm afraid I can't let you do that." I hated that I could only hear one side of the conversation and wished Aiden would put it on speaker. "With all due respect, sir, she's my daughter and I will ensure her safety. Yes, sir." Aiden's head bobbed as he listened, and I made an attempt to grab the phone but he dodged it.

"At least put it on speaker," I demanded.

Aiden did and finally I was able to participate in the conversation.

"Daddy, we're not staying here. It's not safe."

"Sir, she's wrong about that. This is the safest place for her to be."

"Son, I disagree." My father's baritone voice was hard, unyielding. I was grateful that he wasn't changing his mind, but that was short lived. "But I also don't think hopping on a plane is the answer either."

"What?"

"Exactly."

Aiden and I spoke at the same time, causing my father to chuckle.

"Baby girl, this has gone on long enough. Justin isn't going to stop unless someone stops him." A rustling sound came through the line. "Mr. Winters, I've had you checked out." Aiden's face turned bright red. Embarrassment? "It seems you had quite the military career."

"Yes, sir. I, uh… yes, sir." It seems that the General could succeed where his daughter could not. Aiden was unnerved by the fact that he'd been 'checked out'. Knowing his history, I understood, but I also wondered if there was anything I didn't know.

"I sent Scarlett to you before for a reason. I know that she wants to leave, but I'd prefer—"

"Daddy, I'm an adult! You can't make dec—"

"Baby girl, stop." When the General said 'stop', you stopped. "I know I said that I'd get you booked on a flight, but I've changed my mind."

"But—"

"But nothing, Scarlett Rose Runyon." Aiden's brow quirked up at my father's use of my full name. "I sat back and didn't interfere when you wanted to stay in the states for college. I sat back when you were trekking all over God's creation when that lunatic was hunting you. I will not sit back and let you run again."

"Sir, if I may make a suggestion?" Aiden tried to hit the

button to take the call off of speakerphone, but I stopped him. He rolled his eyes at me but didn't try again.

"I'm listening."

"I can protect Scarlett and Tillie, that's true. But I'd prefer it if she were at my place. I have a house that sits on Broken Rebel Brotherhood property, and it's surrounded by acres of nothing. The other members are close by to help out if and when they're needed. No one could get to them there."

"Are you saying that you can't protect her if she remains at her rental?"

"No, sir, not at all." Aiden shook his head as he spoke. "Just that it would be much easier, and safer, for the both of them. I can send you the specs of the security system if you want to see for yourself."

"Ah, son, you assume I haven't already seen them."

"Well, yes, I guess so."

"Like I said, I've done some checking. I've already spoken to Jackson, as well as Micah, Griffin, Brie, Sadie and Doc. I also requested the blueprints to your cabin, as well as the Brotherhood's main house, a sketch of the property and specs for the security system."

"Jesus. You don't mess around." Aiden shoved his free hand through his hair and dropped to the bed.

"When it comes to the safety of my family, no, I don't. Now, Scarlett, are you listening?"

"Yes, Daddy," I huffed. I glared at Aiden, pissed off that he'd taken control of this phone call.

"Still have an attitude, I see." There was censure in my father's voice but there was also love. And that made me smile. "Mr. Winters, I'd like you to take them to your place immediately. I'm sure there will be some sort of cost associated with breaking the lease, and I'll take care of that. Scarlett, don't give him too much lip. He loves you and if you weren't so hell bent on taking care of things on your own, you might be able to admit that you love him too."

Aiden's head whipped up, and his gaze penetrated through to my soul. I chewed on my bottom lip, angry at my dad for saying that but also recognizing the truth to the words. I did love Aiden. Had since the moment he opened his door to me four years ago. But dammit, that declaration should come from me, and I wasn't ready to make it yet.

"Sir—"

"Call me Tom. You're family after all. Even if my daughter is too stubborn to admit it."

"Yes, si... Tom." Aiden's entire demeanor relaxed, and for the first time since he'd walked into Tillie's room to see me packing, he smiled. A genuine smile. "As for breaking the lease, I'm not going to let Scarlett do that." My eyes flew to his, unsure of where he was going with that statement.

"And why not?" Daddy sounded more intrigued than angry.

"You're absolutely right, I do love your daughter, more than anything. Well, more than anything other than my own daughter. And I think you're right. Scarlett does love me." He held up a hand when I opened my mouth to speak. "But that's something that she needs to realize on her own. I don't want them under my roof because they have to be. At least not long term. I'll take them both there, as you requested, and I'll protect them and love them the best way I know how. But when this whole thing is over, it'll be Scarlett's decision if she wants to stay."

"And if she chooses not to stay?"

"Then she and Tillie will have a place to live. And I will make sure that I'm a part of Tillie's life no matter what. Nothing will ever change how I feel about them, but it has to be a hundred percent mutual if we're going to have a life together, as a family." Aiden looked at me and his smile was gone. In its place was a look of determination, conviction. He meant every word he said. "Those are my terms. If you don't agree with them or if you no longer think I'm the right man for your daughter, then I'll put them on a plane myself. It'll be the hardest thing I'll ever do, but I will do it."

"That won't be necessary, son." My father sounded odd, choked up. He was getting soft in his old age. "Your terms are fine with me. But I'm not the one you need to convince."

Aiden looked at me and his gaze landed on the tears snaking their way down my cheeks. He was off the bed in a flash and wiping them away with a swipe of his thumb.

"What do ya say, sugar? You with me or do you still want to run?"

I lowered my head and squeezed my eyes shut to stop the tears. When I was certain that no more would fall, I raised my head and thrust out my chin.

"I'm with you," I whispered.

"Thank God." Aiden wrapped his free arm around my waist and tugged me toward him. He held onto me and peppered my hair with kisses, the phone call with my father momentarily forgotten.

My father cleared his throat, and Aiden jolted away from me. I smothered a laugh with my hand.

"Sorry, sir."

"Son, it's Tom."

"Right. Sorry."

"You'll learn. Now, Scarlett, go get my granddaughter. I'd like to hear her voice. Take your time though. Your man and I are going to get to know each other a bit while you're gone."

Aiden's face paled at that pronouncement, and I chuckled at his unease. I'd spent a lifetime being subjected to my father's questions. It was someone else's turn.

24

AIDEN

Two months had passed since Scarlett's father pronounced that he felt she and Tillie would be safer at my house. Two months since she'd grudgingly agreed. And it had been five weeks since my original 'give me a month to win you over' request had ended.

I'd counted down the days like they were my last on Earth. I loved her, and Tillie, and no amount of time was going to change that. When the month was up, I'd tried to not bring it up, let her come to me, and I'd failed. It had been a normal day, like so many others, and she'd gotten caught up in her routine.

When we'd gone to bed and she still hadn't acknowledged it, I broke down and asked her what she wanted. Her answer? She asked if that decision could be put off until after everything with her ex was over. My response? Even though I'd died a little inside, I agreed.

So there I was, two months of having both her and Tillie under my roof, living together like the family we were, and I was still not sure how things would end up. Thinking about all of it had me seeking out the whiskey while Scarlett put

Tillie to bed. Normally I'd help, but our daughter just wanted her 'mommy' so I left them to it.

I swirled the amber liquid in the tumbler, the ice clinking on the glass. My relationship with Scarlett, or lack thereof, wasn't the only thing on my mind. There hadn't been any more *packages* from Justin, and that set me on edge.

Every day I woke up with warm, soft female—oh yes, she still slept with me despite her indecision—and boiling rage riding shotgun. I'd burn off some of the fury when I was balls deep in Scarlett's welcoming body, but not all of it. It was always there, simmering under the surface, begging to be unleashed. If only Justin would make a move so we could put this shit behind us.

Be careful what you wish for.

Micah's words echoed in my mind. He'd told me that when I'd gone to him and complained about the lack of progress. He was pissed as hell that Justin hadn't been caught, but nobody was as pissed as me. We'd brought Jackson up to speed, but a week later, he was gone. Apparently, the FBI wanted him to start earlier than expected. The interim Sheriff was a douche and no help at all. We were on our own.

I raised my glass to my lips, but it was empty. I scowled as I stood and went to get a refill.

"You planning on getting drunk tonight?"

I stiffened at the accusation in Scarlett's tone before slowly turning from the counter and facing her. Her arms were crossed over her chest, and in the skimpy tank she was wearing, her cleavage was only enhanced by the stance. My cock rose to attention, as it always did around her, no matter how much alcohol was in my system.

"Don't know yet." I rose the glass, in mock solute, and then downed the whiskey in one long gulp. "Kinda looks that way, though." I reached for the bottle, poured myself another and raised it to my lips.

"Kinda looks like you'll be sleeping on the couch." She quirked an eyebrow at me, and her foot began to tap.

Between her attitude and my incurable anger, I lost it. The full glass shattered, and whiskey splashed when I threw it in the sink like a football player spiking the ball after scoring a touchdown.

Don't do this. Don't scare her.

My inner voice was no match for me. I stalked toward her, ignoring the shock on her face at my outburst, and thrust my hands through her hair and pulled her toward me.

I bent down next to her ear. "Sugar, no one's sleeping on the couch," I growled.

Scarlett's lips parted and her head fell back. She knew I wouldn't physically hurt her even if she wasn't convinced I wouldn't break her heart. I nipped at her neck before licking a path down her throat and back up over her chin, landing on her tempting, infuriating mouth.

I thrust my tongue past her tightly sealed lips and she melted. She ran her hands up under my shirt, digging her nails into my pecs. I welcomed the biting pain. I angled my head and kissed her harder. She ground her hips into mine, and I almost combusted at the contact. My hands went from her hair to her ass, holding her to me.

She wrenched her lips away, and her eyes sparked blue fire. "I'm mad at you," she pouted but there was no heat in the statement. Only unabashed lust.

"Does that mean you don't want this?" I knew what her answer would be. I always knew. If I'd crossed a line she wouldn't have let me into her mouth.

"Not a chance." Her expression turned sultry, and her pouty bottom lip begged to be sucked on.

Her hands went to the waistband of my sweats, and as she

pushed them down my thighs, she knelt on the floor. I lifted my feet, one at a time, to help her shed my pants and she tossed them over her shoulder. I glanced down and the sight of her kneeling, her mouth perfectly aligned with my erection, had my dick twitching. I yanked my shirt over my head as the heat in the room ratcheted up twenty degrees.

"Better hold on, soldier," she purred right before she licked my tip and sucked me deep.

I blindly reached behind me, gripped the kitchen counter and threw my head back. Scarlett hummed her way up and down my cock, and I shuddered at the vibrations that went all the way to my toes. Needing to watch, I lowered my head. The moment I laid eyes on the erotic sight of her head bobbing and my length being swallowed up, I groaned.

"So fucking good, sugar."

"Mmmm."

She reached around and grabbed my ass, squeezing and then flattening her hands, her fingers inching their way to the hole that only she was allowed to touch. When they reached their destination and one slender tip penetrated, my balls drew tight and tingles raced down my spine.

"Ahhhh." I shouted out the most intense orgasm of my life, emptying myself into her mouth.

When the shudders ceased and I felt like I could stand without collapsing, I reached down and lifted her up, her lips making a satisfying popping sound when she released me. I watched as she licked her lips and unbelievably, I started to get hard all over again.

I spun us around and trapped her between the counter and my body. She squealed when she hit the cold surface, and in her effort to push away from it, her hips jolted back and slammed into my semi-hard dick.

"Not so fast."

I yanked her tank over her head and tossed it on the floor

and then shoved her skimpy shorts over her hips, letting them fall down her legs. I urged her torso down so her cheek rested on the granite. Her breath came out in choppy pants, and goosebumps broke out over her flushed skin.

I leaned over and flattened my tongue on the base of her spine. She shivered and moaned, letting me know she wanted what I was giving. I licked a path toward her hip, up her side, nipping here and there. When I reached her neck, I sucked, leaving a mark that would serve as a reminder of my passionate assault, at least for a few days.

"Better hold on, sugar." I mimicked her earlier words to me and grinned in satisfaction when her arms stretched over the counter to grip the opposite edge.

I dropped to my knees behind her and stared at her bare ass like I'd never seen it before. She was perfectly sculpted, and I knew the creamy globes would nestle into my groin like they were made for me and me alone.

"Stare too long and I'm gonna have to take care of myself."

Her words snapped me out of my trance, and I chuckled. "Can't have that."

I nudged her legs apart and reached between them to slide a finger through her slit, knowing that the lubrication was necessary. She was wet, and I was tempted to focus all of my attention on what I knew would send her over the edge, but I wanted to play. I slowly teased her ass cheeks, dipping my finger back into her juices every few seconds.

When her moaning morphed into pleading, I penetrated her tight hole with one finger, then two. Scarlett loved ass play, and I knew she could not only handle it but she craved it. A lot. As I teased her with one hand, I reached around with the other and touched her clit, lightly at first and then increasing the pressure. She squirmed and quivered and moved her hips to increase the friction in both places.

"So needy. So wet." My cock was ready again, beyond ready, and feeling her response to me, knowing I'd done that to her, had me reeling.

I withdrew my fingers from her ass and stood, never taking my other hand away from her clit. Scarlett whimpered, begged for my fingers back, but I ignored it. I reached out and fisted a hand in her hair and pulled her up and into me.

"I need you to fuck me. Now, Aiden." She tried to turn around, but I stopped her.

"I'm gonna fuck you, sugar." I swirled my finger over her clit in fast little circles. "Just not quite yet." When her body stiffened, I pulled my finger away and spun her around to face me. Her eyes were wide, and her face flushed. "First, I'm going to make you come all over my hand." I speared her with a thick digit, crooking it to reach that sweet spot. I resumed the torment on her clit with my thumb and enjoyed the look of ecstasy that crossed her face. "And just when you think you're spent and can't take any more?" I increased my speed and her walls began to spasm. "I'm going to shatter you."

She exploded and her muscles sucked my finger until it couldn't go any deeper. I watched as her mouth opened to scream, and then she slammed it shut before any noise came out. Her shaking slowed and her body slowly relaxed. When her knees buckled, I scooped her up and carried her to the couch. I laid her down and brushed her sweat-dampened hair off her face. Her eyes slid closed, and her look of contentment stole my breath.

"Sugar, we aren't done."

Rather than answer, and with her eyes still closed, she gave me a wicked smile.

I straddled her hips, my knees on either side of her, and thanked God that I had an overly large sofa. I leaned down and kissed her cheek, her eyelids, the tip of her nose and finally, her lips. Her arms wound around my neck, and my hands cupped her face. The kiss was slow, deep, overwhelming in its intensity.

I broke the connection and sat back on my heels, staring into her baby blues. I let my knuckles graze her breasts and watched as her nipples peaked. I pinched and tugged them, listening to the sounds she made, trusting her to let me know if anything hurt.

As her breathing became more ragged, I spread my body over hers and let my dick rub her mound. She was wet, ready. I reached between us and took myself in hand, giving a few jerks. Her hips bucked at the friction this created on her clit.

"Please," she begged as she joined her hand with mine and guided me to her opening.

I wanted to slam into her, but I knew if I did, it would be over too soon, despite the fact that I'd already come. Scarlett didn't want to wait, and she thrust her hips up, impaling herself on me. I collapsed at the sensation of her wet heat surrounding me.

"Move, Aiden." She ground her hips against me to encourage my participation.

I'd told her I would shatter her, not expecting her to turn the tables on me. I lifted myself up onto my hands, braced them on either side of her head, and moved. I pulled out and slammed back in, the sound of our bodies crashing fueling me. Scarlett met me, thrust for thrust, neither of us slowing the pace.

Her muscles spasmed, once, twice, and that tell-tale tingle started in my back. When her body stiffened and she started to milk me, I lost it. I threw my head back, felt the veins in my neck distend and my muscles tense. I spilled into her like

I'd done so many times before, but somehow this was different. More intense. More... everything.

When we both settled, my arms buckled and I managed to twist as I fell so I landed next to her, rather than crushing her with my weight. She rolled so her back was to my front, and I curled my body around hers and wrapped an arm around her waist, pulling her back toward me. I wiggled my other arm under her head and bent close to her ear.

"You are incredible," I whispered.

"Mmm, so are you."

She linked her fingers with mine and nestled closer. It wasn't lost on me that the most powerful sex was born out of anger, but the anger was dead. For now. In its place was a weird sort of calm.

I listened as her breathing evened out and she went lax in my embrace. I pressed a kiss to her temple and mumbled, "Guess I'll be sleeping on the couch, after all."

25

SCARLETT

"*S*hit!"

The panic in Aiden's voice pulled me from a delicious dream. I scrambled from the couch and whirled around to see him do the same.

"What's wrong?" I asked, looking in all directions, trying to determine why he was freaking out.

"We're naked," he exclaimed.

I glanced down at myself and then back up to take in the sight of him, every sexy inked muscle. Soft material smacked me in the face, and I grabbed it, realizing that he'd thrown the blanket from the back of the sofa at me.

"I can't believe I'm saying this, but cover up." He groaned. Actually groaned like a child having his favorite toy taken away. He wrapped the other fleece throw around his waist, and *I* groaned. "Thank fuck Tillie's a heavy sleeper."

He shoved a hand through his hair and stepped around me to trudge to the kitchen. He picked up his clothes, then mine and brought them back to me. I tracked his movement, my hand over my mouth to hide my giggles.

"You think this is funny?" He bent his knees to bring

himself to eye level and scowled. "This isn't funny. She'd be traumatized!"

I lost it. Actually doubled over and lost the battle. What had started out as a tiny giggle became hilarious laughter. And that only served to frustrate him more. When I got myself under control, I stood up straight and one look at him had me laughing again until tears streamed down my face.

"I'm so glad I can amuse you," he mumbled as he stomped away like a petulant child and went upstairs.

I didn't bother with my clothes, but rather stayed wrapped in the blanket as I followed him. When I entered the bedroom, the one we had shared since Tillie and I moved in, I heard the shower running. I turned around and retraced my steps as far as Tillie's room, peeked in and satisfied myself that she was still sleeping and then joined Aiden in the shower.

"Are you done pouting?" I asked as I soaped up my hands and fisted his dick.

He was hard as a rock, and it was more than morning wood. He seemed to always be hard when I was around, but I wasn't complaining.

"Maybe."

He lifted me up and pressed me into the shower wall. My legs wrapped around his waist, and my arms held onto his neck. He thrust inside me, and it wasn't long before we were both climaxing. My ears rang, my body trembled and he held on, making sure I didn't crumble. Spent, we washed up and got dressed for the day.

A look at the clock told me it was time to wake Tillie up and get her ready. Apparently, she woke up on the wrong side of the bed because her attitude that morning was epic. She didn't want to wear the outfit I'd laid out the night before. She didn't want to eat the breakfast that Aiden made and begged for ice cream. By the time we left, I was more than ready for a break.

I dropped her off at pre-school and then returned home. When I'd started thinking of Aiden's place as my home, I had no idea, but I liked it. The time with him had been amazing and I'd realized, several days in, that I was more than a little in love with him. Though I hadn't told him. I wanted this thing with Justin to be over first. I didn't want any of that to touch any of this.

Aiden left me a note saying he would be at Micah's if I needed anything. I didn't, so I spent most of the morning relaxing and binging on some Netflix. At some point, I'd fallen asleep and woke up to the sound of my phone beeping.

Thinking it was my reminder that it was time to pick Tillie up, I let it beep, knowing it would eventually stop. I turned the television off and went to grab my purse and keys off the kitchen counter. On my way back through the living room, I swiped my cell off the coffee table and out the door I went.

My phone beeped again, several times, and after starting the car, I finally tapped the cell's screen and cleared any notifications. When I glanced at it, the first thing that I noticed was that it was way too early to pick Tillie up. Frowning, I stared at the device, trying to figure out why it'd been beeping. That's when I noticed the little red five at the corner of the text icon.

I tapped the little green box and screamed.

∼

"This can't be happening. Not my baby girl. Ohmygod."

I mumbled, over and over, as I drove to Micah's. Fortunately, it wasn't far because no doubt I'd have wrecked the car if I had to go on main roads. Part of me thought to call the cops, but with the new Sheriff, I wasn't so certain that was a good idea. I just had to get to Aiden. He'd know what to do.

I slammed the car in park and skidded to a halt in the driveway and sent gravel flying. I laid on the horn, hoping to pull Aiden and the others outside. In seconds, he, Micah and Griffin tore out the front door and down the steps.

Aiden yanked open my door and bent to look me in the eye. "Scarlett, what's wrong? What happened?"

I took in his fierce protectiveness, stubborn jaw, tense muscles, everything. We'd been so happy, content and that was ruined now. I didn't bother hiding my tears as I picked up my phone from the passenger seat and brought it to life so Aiden could see the picture.

"Fuck!" he roared as his fists crashed down on the hood of the car. He yanked the device out of my hand and showed Micah and Griffin.

"Son of a bitch," Micah muttered as he stared wide-eyed at the picture of Tillie, hands and feet bound and duct tape over her mouth.

I didn't need to look at it again to see the scared expression on her face, the tears that had tracked through dirt on her cheeks, her mussed hair. That image was burned into my brain and would never be forgotten.

"C'mon, Scarlett, let's get you inside." Aiden reached down and helped me out of the vehicle, holding me steady as we walked inside.

I was guided to what appeared to be an office. Griffin immediately got to work on the computer while Micah and Aiden pulled out maps of the area. They were a flurry of activity around me, but I barely noticed. Flashes of memory assaulted me, one after the other. All the middle of the night fleeing, all the bedtime stories and morning routines. Every single second of Tillie's life seemed to race their way through my mind at warp speed. With the shift of each image, the crying slowed and blind fury took the place of sadness.

I shot out of the chair, intent on leaving, finding Justin and murdering him. Aiden snaked his arm out and stopped me from crossing the threshold.

"Scarlett, stop." There was a hard edge to his voice, one that couldn't be ignored. He stepped in front of me and placed his hands on my shoulders. "We'll find her and make him pay. I promise. But you have to trust me. I can't have you going off halfcocked, giving me one more thing to worry about."

"I can't sit here and do nothing. Don't you dare ask that of me," I seethed. "She's my daughter."

"She's *our* daughter and we'll bring her home." He urged me to turn back around.

"I need to do something, any—"

Aiden's phone rang, and he pulled it out of his pocket. His shoulders stiffened when he glanced at the screen and then he answered, putting it on speakerphone.

"You're a dead man," he pushed out through his clenched teeth.

"Threats? Really?" Justin's voice came through the speaker, and my heart plummeted to the floor. He sounded cold but cocky. A deadly combination. "Is that any way to talk to the man that has—"

"I want to talk to her," Aiden interrupted. "Let me talk to her and this will go a lot better for you."

"No can do." Justin's laugh was mocking, hollow. "You'll just have to trust me that she's alive. For now."

My hand flew to my mouth to stifle my cries, but it was futile.

"Ah, Scarlett, I knew you'd be there." Justin sounded pleased with himself. "I couldn't have planned this any better if I tried." There was a rustling that came over the line, like he was moving something heavy, and I couldn't stop my thoughts from racing. "Here's what's going to happen. You listening?"

I nodded and then realized that he couldn't see me.

"Ye-yes," I stuttered. "I'll do anything you want. I just want Tillie back."

"Well, you've got one thing right. You will do anything I want, but you won't get Tillie back." He paused and when he spoke again, it was like he was a different person. The person who had beat me bloody and left me for dead. "She's my daughter and yet, you let that overgrown ape play daddy. I couldn't just sit back and do nothing." He took a deep breath. "We could've been so happy. We were happy once, right?"

I didn't answer, not sure how to respond to the ramblings of a madman. Besides, how was I supposed to tell him what he wants to hear when just the thought of the lies made me what to vomit?

Aiden covered the phone and leaned in to whisper, "Tell him what he wants to hear."

I gave a curt nod. I'd do it, tell him the lies, say whatever if it meant getting Tillie back.

"We were happy. And we can be again. Just tell me where you are, and I'll meet you." The words were acid on my tongue, but I ignored it. "The three of us can go somewhere and start over."

"See, that's the thing. How am I supposed to believe that when even you don't believe it? How am I supposed to just forget that I had to hunt you down?"

"I'm sorry. It was a mistake. All of it. I never should have left you. I won't ever do it again."

"We'll see about that. For now, I only have one thing left to say to ape boy."

"What's that?" Aiden asked.

"Your life as you've known it since I left that gift for you in the hospital parking lot is over."

The line went dead.

Blood whooshed through my veins, throbbed in my head. Black spots danced in front of me and my vision blurred.

"Scarlett?" Aiden's voice sounded thick, worried. "Scarlett, sugar, stay with me."

Hands settled at my waist and the room spun. I tried to hold onto consciousness, tried to shove the darkness away.

"Goddamnit!"

Aiden's exclamation was punctuated with a loud crash, and I surrendered. Let myself be sucked into an abyss that was as cold and dark as Justin's heart.

26

AIDEN

"*I* got it."

I sat on the edge of the couch in Micah's living room, next to Scarlett. When she'd lost consciousness, I'd scooped her up and carried her there.

"Got what?" I brushed a wispy strand of hair off of Scarlett's forehead before pressing a kiss to her cheek and rising to face Griffin.

"His location."

Griffin seemed pleased with himself, but I couldn't quite bring myself to be happy about the information. Not when my daughter was out there, scared, and the love of my life lay motionless.

"Aiden, this is good." Griffin slapped me on the back as he shoved his tablet in front of my face. I glanced at the map on the screen and narrowed my eyes. "See the red dot? That's where they are."

I glanced over my shoulder at Scarlett and took in her pale face. My fists clenched at my sides and my blood boiled. I wanted to storm out of the house right then, but we'd agreed that we needed a plan.

"Why would anyone do this? She's just a little girl."

"People are fucked up," Micah said simply as he entered the room. He'd called Sadie and asked her to come home to sit with Scarlett while we went and got Tillie back. "Sadie's on her way. Should be here in ten."

"We don't have ten minutes." Scarlett's voice was quiet, and my head whipped around to see her struggling to sit up. I didn't go to her, I couldn't. Not when I was wound that tightly.

"What she said," I raged, all of my emotions no longer able to be kept in check. "I need to go now." I rounded the couch and headed for the door.

"Aiden, stop," Micah commanded. "You go alone and you're likely to get yourself killed."

His lack of confidence in my ability to handle myself pissed me off even more. "I. Can't. Wait."

Micah and I faced off, both unyielding in our stares. Scarlett stood and placed herself in between the two of us, as if she could stop us if we were so inclined to actually fight. I huffed out a breath just as the door behind me opened and Sadie walked in and stopped in her tracks at the sight before her.

"I see I made it just in time."

"Sweetness, we have to go. Will you and Scarlett be okay here?"

"I'm not staying behind." Scarlett whirled on Micah, and her anger was impressive.

She was in full mama bear mode. But she was wrong. I couldn't have her in the way. And I certainly couldn't have her be a witness to whatever violence took place. Because there would be violence. Lots of it if I had my way. She didn't need to see that side of me.

"Sugar, he's right. You need to stay here. It's too dangerous," I pleaded.

"And the last four years haven't been?" she yelled. "I can handle myself." With that, she stormed past me and out the door.

"I like her." Griffin said as he followed Scarlett, leaving Micah and I standing there, glaring at their backs.

"Jesus, this is going to be a shit show," I mumbled as I strode out the door.

Scarlett and Griffin were both in the Jeep, Griffin in the driver's seat. I yanked the door open and glowered at him.

"I'm driving."

Griffin didn't argue, just got out and moved to the back seat, where Scarlett was sitting. Micah got in the passenger's side, and I took off before he could even get the door shut.

As I drove, Griffin called out directions based on the GPS. It appeared that Justin was at the old Ford plant in the next town over. The blinking red dot hadn't moved, and the closer we got to it, the harder I gripped the wheel, ready to rescue Tillie. Ready to pound Justin into oblivion.

The Jeep skidded to a halt in front of the run-down building, and I took in my surroundings. All of my training came flooding back. I was no longer a father from rural Indiana. I was a Navy Seal on a rescue mission.

We all got out of the vehicle and Griffin, Micah and I got our gear out of the back: bullet-proof vests, guns, flashlights, anything we could possibly need and everything we could carry. Scarlett reached for the Sig Sauer P238, the only weapon remaining. My eyebrows shot up in surprise when she popped the clip, checked for bullets and readied the weapon. Her confidence and ability was sexy as fuck but that wasn't the time.

"Let's do this." I headed toward the back of the building to a less visible entrance. Justin wasn't expecting us but no need to tip him off by breaking in the front.

When we entered the plant, Scarlett and I went in one

direction while Micah and Griffin went in another. We swept the entire building. No Tillie and no Justin. It was obvious that they'd been there. A half full Styrofoam cup of coffee sat on the floor in one corner. It was lukewarm, telling me they'd only left recently. Next to the cup was balled up duct tape and a children's book.

We reconvened at the Jeep and spread out a map of the county. There were plenty of places that Justin could take her, hide her, and we wouldn't stop until we'd searched every last one.

"Now what?" Scarlett slid the Sig Sauer into the back of her waistband, way too comfortable with a firearm than I cared to admit, because admitting that would be admitting that she'd needed one in the first place.

"Call him," Griffin suggested.

"And say what? We found your little hideout and are coming for you? That'll only piss him off, and he could take it out on Tillie." I shoved a hand through my hair before whirling around and punching the door of the Jeep. The pain didn't even register. I threw my head back and shouted into the sky, needing to release myself of some of the pent-up rage.

"I'll call him." Scarlett dug her phone out of her pocket and pulled up the text messages from earlier. "I can tell him I want to meet him. Leave with him. Maybe he'll give me his location." Her expression gave away the fact that she didn't believe it would work but we were desperate.

"It's worth a shot." Micah tossed his weapons into the cargo hold and turned to Griffin. "Get your laptop, see if we can trace the call."

Griffin pulled up the necessary software while Scarlett paced, waiting for the go-ahead.

I stepped in front of her and rubbed my hands up and

down her arms. She rested her hands on my chest and drew in a deep breath before she spoke.

"I need you to know, that no matter what happens—"

"Okay, Scarlett, you can call him." Griffin sat in the Jeep, turned sideways with his feet firmly on the ground and his computer balanced on his lap. "Keep him on the phone as long as you can."

With a shaky hand, she made the call, keeping it on speakerphone. One ring, two rings, three rings. After the sixth ring, I was sure that he was fucking with us. Finally, the ringing stopped.

"Mommy?"

Scarlett's knees buckled at the sound of Tillie's voice, and I reached out to hold her up. When she was steady, she spoke.

"Hi baby." Her breath hitched and she paused to gain control of her emotions, not wanting to scare our daughter. "Are you okay?"

"Mommy, I scared." Tillie sounded like she'd been crying, and I vowed to take every tear out of Justin's hide.

"I know baby, but mommy and daddy are coming for you, okay."

"Hey, peanut."

"Daddy, I wanna come home."

Those words pierced my heart, and my eyes began to burn. I wanted to reassure her, tell her how much she was loved, how much better my life was with her and her mother in it, but I did none of those things. Instead, I focused on the mission.

"Peanut, do you know where you are?"

Tillie began sobbing and another muffled voice could be heard, though I couldn't make out the words. After a long moment, silence. I glanced at the screen to see if the call had been dropped, but it was still active.

"Tillie? Baby, talk to me," Scarlett begged.

"Tillie can't come to the phone right now." Justin laughed but there was no humor in it. "What do you want?"

"I, uh, called to see if we could meet. We, um, can be a family. The three of us."

"You mean the four of us?"

"What? No." She violently shook her head as she spoke. "I—"

"Don't lie to me!" Justin raged. An image of him standing over Tillie, body rigid, spit flying from his mouth, came to mind. "Listen to me and listen carefully."

"I'm listening." Scarlett dropped her head in defeat.

"I know you tracked us to the Ford plant." My head whipped around to look at Micah and Griffin, silently asking them how the fuck that was possible. They both shrugged. My mind churned with possibilities as he continued to rant. "I only want one thing. Well, maybe two."

"You can have whatever you want as long as I get Tillie back."

"That's not how this works. Now, if you'll let me finish?"

"Go ahead."

"I want us to be together, you and me." I noticed that he didn't mention Tillie in that equation. "Like we're meant to be."

"Okay." Scarlett dragged the word out, not commenting on the fact that Tillie wasn't included. "What's the second thing?"

"I want to ruin Aiden Winters' life, like he did mine."

Once again, the line went dead after that ominous statement.

Scarlett's eyes locked on mine. "What does he mean 'like he did mine'?" She shook her head as if to sort it out. "I don't know what he means."

"He wants to take away Aiden's daughter, like he thinks Aiden did to him." Micah spoke quietly but with conviction.

I knew what he meant and was grateful that he didn't spell it out in detail. Justin was going to kill Tillie. If he couldn't have her, no one could. Sick fuck.

"But Aiden didn't take Justin's daughter. Tillie's not even *his* daughter! This makes no sense."

"Honey, he's certifiable. It's never going to make sense to those of us who are sane." Griffin stepped up to the other side of Scarlett, laptop in hand. "Here," he turned the computer so I could see it. "I was able to trace the call and then hack into the phone so we could track him. He's on the move."

We piled into the SUV and I gunned the engine. Griffin sat in front this time while Micah sat with Scarlett. I heard him talking to her but couldn't make out the words. Whatever it was, I'm sure it was exactly the right thing to say. He had a knack for that.

We drove for hours, following that damn blinking dot. Every time we got close, the direction would shift, and my anger would heighten. Every minute, every hour, was pure torture and when it got dark, it seemed we'd never catch up. The clock mocked me with every changed digit.

"He stopped," Griffin exclaimed, sometime later. He turned the laptop screen toward me. "Look."

I quickly glanced at it and breathed a sigh of relief, although it was short-lived. Griffin was right and the dot *had* stopped but, why? What did Justin have up his sleeve?

I pulled the Jeep to the side of the road. I didn't want to get too close and spook him. We'd go the rest of the way on foot.

"What the hell?" Micah muttered when we exited the vehicle, and he looked at the map.

"What?" Scarlett asked.

"Why is he stopped on a bridge?"

No one answered the question, not out loud. In my head, warning bells jangled, and I thought 'nothing good'.

We geared up and set off toward Justin. Toward Tillie. It was pitch black out and the middle of the night. There was no traffic, which meant no witnesses for what was about to happen. And no help, should we need it. We probably should have called in the law, but with Jackson gone, it was better this way. No lines to worry about crossing.

When we reached the bridge, the lone streetlight cast an eerie glow. It lit up the rusted metal railings of the bridge like a spotlight on centerstage. And in the spotlight was Tillie, being lifted up by BRB's most wanted.

I took off, running toward them, raising my gun as I went. The others were right behind me.

"I'd stop if I were you," Justin shouted. His words echoed in the wind, amplifying the intensity of the situation.

I skidded to a stop, about 25 yards from them. I didn't want to set him off, make him do something stupid. Justin put Tillie on the railing, and her short little legs dangled over the side. He fisted his hand in her shirt, at her back and held on.

My heart hammered in my chest, threatened to burst through my skin. Sweat poured down my back and pooled at the base of my spine. Tillie's crying reached my ears, and I tightened my grip on my weapon.

"Here's how this is going to work," Justin yelled. "You and your goons are gonna drop your weapons. Scarlett's going to walk to me, slowly, and you're gonna let her. When she's within my reach, I'll let the brat go."

"Not gonna happen," I shouted back. No way was he getting Scarlett. I did lower my weapon, though, confident that Griffin and Micah would take a shot if it came to that.

Out of the corner of my eye, Scarlett walked past me.

"Sugar, don't," I commanded. I reached out, gripped her arm and hauled her back to me.

She looked at me with sad eyes. Determined eyes. "I told you I'd do whatever I had to." Tears streamed down her face, and her bottom lip trembled. "Promise me you won't let her forget me? You'll make sure she knows how much I love her?" She reached up and cupped my cheek with her hand. "Aiden, promise me."

"Dammit, Scarlett, don't do this. You don't have to sacrifice yourself to save her."

"I can see you, ya know?" Scarlett winced at Justin's words. "Hurry it up before I change my mind."

"Please, Aiden. I need to know you'll do this for me."

"I promise." I relented but my mind was already searching for ways to stop this, save them both.

Scarlett swiped at the tears on her cheek and nodded. When she turned and started walking toward her hunter, I noticed that her back was straight and her shoulders squared. She wasn't showing her fear to him. Pride swelled and my chest constricted.

This couldn't be happening. I was losing before I even had a chance to play the game. I looked over my shoulder at my brothers, my family, and knew in that moment that they would get me through this. Them and Tillie.

I turned back around and watched Scarlett as she continued her walk on the proverbial plank. When she reached Justin and he yanked her toward him, my blood boiled.

"I'm here, right where you want me." I heard Scarlett's words and was amazed at her calm. "Let Tillie go."

Justin looked at Tillie and an evil smile spread across his face. Time seemed to stand still, and flurry of activity happened all at once.

Justin released Tillie's shirt and shoved her.

Tillie screamed.

Gunfire exploded.

Scarlett lunged toward our daughter and screamed.

I shouted and took off running.

Before I even had a chance to question my actions, I was flying through the air.

Freezing cold water splashed around me, and my lungs seized. The blackness sucked me in and my last thought before it swallowed me whole was *I failed them.*

27

SCARLETT

"Ma'am, I need to make sure you're not injured."

I stared straight ahead, not seeing a damn thing. I didn't want to be checked for injuries. I wanted to be left alone, wanted to die so I could be with them.

"Scarlett, c'mon honey." A small hand touched my arm, and I jerked away. "Let them look you over so you're ready when Aiden and Tillie wake up."

I spared a glance for Brie, who'd arrived at the hospital with Sadie shortly after their husbands and I did.

"You don't wake up from dead," I sneered.

I gave up the fight and let them steer me toward a curtained off ER bed. When I sat, I recognized activity around me but chose to ignore it. Being in a hospital brought back too many awful memories, and I didn't want to face them. Problem was, you don't always get what you want.

"She's in shock and she's got a nasty lump on her head where she hit the pavement." A light flickered in front of my face, and I realized that they were checking my pupils.

Several minutes of poking and prodding later and I heard someone say, "Other than that, she seems to be fine."

Fine? I was *not* fine. I'd never be *fine* again. Not without my baby. Not without Aiden. Cold infused my bones and I shivered. I wrapped my arms around my body and tried to bury myself in them. Bury myself where no one would ever find me.

"Any updates on Aiden and Tillie?" Again with the voices that were familiar, yet so unwelcome. And with the pointless questions.

"I'll go check on them and find out what I can." Footsteps sounded around me, and suddenly it was silent.

Finally, I was alone. A sob crept up my throat, and I didn't bother to suppress it. There was no build up. There was no warning for the power that tore through me. I sobbed so hard it hurt and so long that I fought to breathe. A grieving mother was an impressive thing.

"Scarlett, look at me."

The command penetrated the thick fog of emotions. After my epic meltdown, I had no strength left to force the world away. I raised my head and took in Micah's concern.

"I need you to listen to me." He took a step toward me and reached out to brush my tears away. "I need you to hear what I'm saying."

I nodded, weakly agreeing despite knowing that whatever he had to say wouldn't matter.

"Good girl." He sat next to me on the bed and picked up my hand, holding it tightly in his much larger one. "Tillie's going to be fine. They've got her set up in a room and treating her like a princess." I whipped my head toward him, and my eyes widened. "You heard me. She's going to be fine."

"But…"

"But nothing." He shook his head. "I know you thought the worst, and I hate that I couldn't be there to make sure you knew what was going on, but I had to focus on… other things."

"She's going to be okay? You mean it?"

"Promise."

My shoulders sagged and overwhelming relief swept through me. Then I remembered I'd been grieving for two people, and it threatened to suck me back under.

"He'll never see her grow up." Tears spilled over my lashes, and Micah wiped them away, patiently.

"Yes, he will." He squeezed my hand, and I looked up at him with questions in my eyes. "He's going to be fine, too. 'Course he's gonna be pissed off that he didn't get to end Justin himself." He chuckled. "But he'll get over that."

"Justin's dead?" So much information was coming at me so fast it was hard to keep up.

"Yep. Put a bullet in him myself."

Tillie was alive. Aiden was alive. Justin was dead.

Now what?

"I was going to ask you the same thing." Micah's statement made me realize I'd spoken the question out loud.

"I, um, I'd like to see them, if I can."

"Of course. They were given adjacent rooms and I'll take you to them in a minute." Micah stood and faced me. "But first I need to tell you something."

"Okay."

"Be damn sure of what you want." At my questioning look he continued. "Aiden loves you, and he loves Tillie. So much so that we almost lost him tonight." He took a few deep breaths. "He'd kill me for this, but I can live with that. What I can't live with is watching him go through the motions, day in and day out, slowly killing himself with bad decisions. You broke his heart once before. And if there is even the slightest doubt in your mind or heart that he's who you want to spend the rest of your life with, walk away now. When Tillie's released, take her and be happy. But don't keep giving him false hope and then disappear. I'm not sure he'd survive it a second time."

"The last thing I want to do is hurt him."

"I know. Doesn't mean you won't." Micah bent over and kissed the top of my head before turning and walking away.

I sat there, replaying his words in my head on a loop. My heart was so full, and I was beyond happy knowing that Tillie and Aiden were okay. Was I ready to risk that feeling? Was I ready to move on and trust that life could be sweet from here on out?

The answer slammed into me. One thousand percent yes. I loved Aiden. Had for years despite trying to fight it. So much devastation could have been avoided if I'd trusted him in the first place. He'd shown me in hundreds of ways how he felt about me, about Tillie. I couldn't walk away, not again.

I stood, feeling like the weight of the world had been lifted off of my shoulders, and walked to the waiting room. Micah was there, as was Griffin, Sadie, Brie, Doc and so many others. All eyes turned to me but only one of them approached.

"You're staying," Micah said.

"How'd you know?"

"Your face says it all." He shrugged. "Ready to go see Tillie?"

"God, yes."

I followed him to the elevator, and we rode to the third floor in silence. When we exited, Tillie's voice reached me, and I raced down the hallway toward the sound. I found her room and ran to her bedside and scooped her up.

"Oh baby, I was so scared." I held her tight, never wanting to let go again.

"Uh, Scarlett, you might want to put her down," Micah

was beside me, chuckling. That's when the beeping monitors registered.

I laid Tillie back down and covered her with the blanket just as two nurses flew into the room.

"Sorry, I got excited." I wiped away my tears, happy ones, and laughed at myself.

"Mommy, why you cwying?"

The nurses checked the machines and satisfied that Tillie was fine, they left.

"Baby, I'm just so happy you're okay."

"I was scared but daddy was there. He saved me." Out of the mouths of babes.

"Yeah, he did."

Micah left Tillie and I alone for a while, and I sat with her until she fell asleep. Satisfied that I could leave her for a bit, I walked out of the room and ran smack dab into Micah.

"Whoa," he said, and his arms shot out to steady me. "You okay?"

I nodded frantically. "Where is he?"

"In there." He hitched his thumb over his shoulder indicating Aiden's room.

I took a deep breath and blew it out before standing on my tiptoes to kiss Micah's cheek. "Thanks, Micah."

"For what?" He shifted on his feet, uncomfortable.

"For everything." I lowered my gaze for a brief second before looking him in the eyes. "But most of all, for not letting me suffocate in my grief. For making me see."

I stepped around him and walked toward my future.

28

AIDEN

"Sir, I need you to sit still."

"And I need to get out of this damn bed."

I'd woken up to realize I was in the hospital. In a fucking backless gown. I hated hospitals, and it seemed that I'd been in them an awful lot lately. I glared at the nurse as she checked my IV, hoping to scare her. It didn't work.

"Quit the macho man routine. I've dealt with some pretty scary men, and I hate to break it to you, but you don't even rank in the top twenty."

She walked around the bed to check a monitor and then made notations on a chart. I watched her every move, mentally willing her away.

"I'll be back in a bit to check on you." The nurse finally started toward the door.

"Wait," I called to her back.

She slowly turned around and raised an eyebrow. "Now you want me here." She chuckled and shook her head. "What can I do for you?"

"You can give me answers." The words came out angrier

than I'd intended. "Please, I need to know what happened to everyone else at the bridge."

"I'm sorry, honey. I don't know." Her expression softened. "Tell ya what. I'll go do some checking, and if I can find anything out, I'll let you know."

"Thanks." It would have to be good enough.

When she left the room, my thoughts spiraled. Images flashed and sounds erupted in my head. Justin yelling. Tillie crying. Scarlett sacrificing herself for our daughter. Her walking away from me. Tillie falling through the air. Gunshots. Me running, jumping, crashing into nothingness. Nothing made sense.

No one would tell me anything, and I'd asked every new person I saw. I asked question after question. Was Tillie found? What happened to Scarlett? Was Justin arrested? Where were my brothers? How were they? The answer was always the same. I don't know.

"Fuck," I roared to the empty room.

"I figured you'd be happier to see me."

My gaze shot toward the voice, and my breath caught in my throat. I rubbed my chest and blinked my eyes, sure I was seeing things.

"Aiden?"

It was Scarlett's voice. Scarlett's body that seemed to float on the air and come closer. I was losing it. *Floating?* Was she a ghost?

"No," she answered the question I hadn't realized I'd said out loud. When she was close enough, she reached out and picked up my hand. "I'm real."

"How? I watched you walk away. You were next to him." I shook my head. "He pushed Tillie." Fury replaced confusion, and I sat up and tried to swing my legs over the bed.

"Stop." Scarlett urged me back down. "Tillie's fine."

"But…"

"That was pretty much the same reaction I had." She grazed my cheek with her fingertips. "I promise, she's okay. She's in the room next door."

One fear put to rest. Just as quickly, another hit.

"Justin? Where's Justin."

"Dead."

"How?"

"Micah shot him." She said that as if taking someone's life was the most natural thing in the world.

"Fucker." I'd wanted to kill him but hadn't even been able to do that right.

"He said you'd be pissed. Also said you'd get over it."

"He lied." I dropped my head, shame overtaking me at not being able to protect her and Tillie. At not being good enough to keep evil out of their lives. When I looked back up at her, tears were swimming in my eyes. "I'm so sorry."

"For what?" She cocked her head.

"I broke my promise. I didn't keep you both safe."

"Aiden, stop." She crawled onto the bed and laid down beside me, resting her head on my chest. "You did nothing wrong and everything right. There's no figuring out crazy so let's stop trying. It's over. It's finally over."

I wanted to believe her, to know in my soul that she believed what she said. But something held me back. And because of that, I told myself that she was better off without me. I tried to push her away before she could do it to me.

"I guess you'll be leaving soon, heading back to... I don't even know where you lived before this."

"All over the place." I felt her shrug. "Don't really have anywhere to go back to." A sliver of hope emerged, but I pushed it away. "Besides, even if I had somewhere to go, who says I wanna leave?"

Don't get your hopes up.

"I just thought... I mean, surely—"

"Shut up, Aiden."

"Excuse me?"

"You heard me." She lifted herself up to look me in the eye. "I'm not going anywhere. Tillie and I are staying here."

"Oh, great. When I'm released, um, I can help you settle back in at the rental."

"Is that what you want?"

"No." I didn't even try to lie, not to her. I could tell myself a million different things to make this hurt less, but I could never lie to her.

"What do you want, Aiden?"

I wasn't sure what answer she was hoping to get, but again, I couldn't lie. I pushed a strand of hair behind her ear, and she leaned into my touch.

"I want it all."

"Me too," she whispered. "I love you so much, Aiden Winters. When I thought you were gone, that Tillie was gone, I wanted to die just to be with you."

"Sugar, a little crazy and some water can't hurt me," I chided. Then *all* of her words registered. "Wait. What did you say?"

"Wondered how long it would take you."

"What. Did. You. Say?"

"I love you. I have loved you for years, and I will love you for always."

"Are you sure?" I asked, not quite able to believe it. "If you're not, walk away now."

"What is it with you men?" she huffed and when I quirked a brow at her, she continued. "Micah said the same damn thing."

"I'll kill him," I growled.

She smiled and rested her forehead against mine. "No, you won't. You love him," she said simply. "Anyway, you're not going to live long enough to kill him if you don't tell me you love me too."

Not wanting to die, I said, "I love you too." And just because, I said, "I will spend every single day for the rest of my life making sure you never forget it."

"I have no doubt."

"And I'll spend just as long being the father Tillie deserves."

"You already are."

"But first…"

"Yeah?"

"Fucking kiss me already."

And she did. For quite a while.

It still wasn't enough.

EPILOGUE

SCARLETT

Two years later...

"One more good push."

The doctor's encouraging words let us know it was almost over. Excitement buzzed in the hallway as new life was brought into the world. Men cheered, woman cried. It was contagious.

A piercing cry split the air and a chorus of cheers erupted. Aiden hugged me, the whole experience making him emotional. Griffin stepped into the hall, and all eyes turned to him.

In his arms was a tiny bundle wrapped in blue. There was a light in his eyes that only came from holding your child in your arms for the first time. I glanced at Aiden and recognized the envy in his gaze. He'd never say it out loud, but he wanted to experience that.

"Everyone, I'd like you to meet Liam Aiden Strong." Griffin's chest puffed out with pride and Aiden's head snapped up. Griffin shrugged. "You're my best friend. And his godfather."

"Seriously?" Aiden asked.

"Well, yeah. And Scarlett, we're hoping you'll be his godmother." Griffin smiled down at Liam and brushed his fingertips over his son's cheek.

"I'd be honored."

Everyone took turns cooing over the new baby for a few minutes before Griffin took him back to Brie. As things died down, I silently slipped away and down the hall to the waiting area, where I dropped into a chair.

Sitting there, alone, I thought back over everything that had happened over the last few years. The horrific events that led me to this place, with these people. To feeling so full of light and love.

After Aiden and Tillie were released from the hospital, we returned to his place and broke my lease. It was difficult to move past that night that the world seemed to stop. I had nightmares. Tillie had nightmares. And every time, Aiden was there to hold us together, bring us back out of the darkness.

There'd been an investigation into the death of Justin, but it hadn't lasted long. The new Sheriff dragged his feet for six months until one day, the questions stopped. We suspected that Jackson had pulled some strings, but no one had talked to him so we couldn't know for sure.

When we were able to completely put everything behind us, Aiden proposed. I looked at the ring on my finger, the diamond as mesmerizing as it was the day he gave it to me. He'd told me that he'd had the ring for years, that he'd been planning to pop the question before I'd gotten pregnant and left. No one could confirm this, although Griffin said it was likely true. It didn't matter. All that mattered was that I said yes, and we were married six months later.

The wedding was supposed to be a small, intimate affair, but turned into a giant party. My parents flew in for the wedding, and my father and Aiden immediately hit it off. Not that I was worried. Military men, no matter what branch, tended to stick together.

The entire Broken Rebel Brotherhood was in attendance, all one hundred and seventy-eight members. The Brotherhood has grown a lot since it was formed. There were now chapters all over the country and more member requests every day. The original five had still remained on the main property, running things and helping out with cases, but their main focus was their families.

"Sugar, I was looking for you." Aiden sat in the chair next to me and picked up my hand and placed a kiss on my knuckles. "I was worried when I turned around and you were gone."

"Sorry. I didn't mean to worry you." I sniffled, not having realized that my thoughts had caused tears.

"Why are you crying? You know I can't stand it when you cry. You or Tillie. It guts me."

"I know. But I'm happy, so it's okay."

"I never did understand that. Crying when you're happy? That's stupid."

I laughed at him and he swiped my tears away.

"I was just thinking about how much life has changed. How good it is."

"It is pretty amazing." He leaned back in his chair and rested his head against the wall. "I sat just like this the night the hospital called me. The night I found out about Tillie."

"Yeah?"

"Yep. I was sure I was going to fuck things up." He sat up and pinned me with his gaze. "I know I'm not perfect, but I don't think I've fucked up too bad. Not yet anyway."

"You definitely haven't fucked up." I leaned in and kissed

him. Our kisses were always explosive, and I had to pull away before I jumped him right then and there.

"How about we head home and relieve the babysitter? I bet Tillie's dying to hear about the new baby."

"I wouldn't be so sure. Isaiah and Izzy are there, and you know how inseparable they've become."

Aiden grunted, not liking his daughter around any boys. It didn't seem to matter that they were only seven and spent most of their time playing hide and seek. He stood and tugged me up with him.

"We need to go." He pulled me toward the elevator, but I dug in my heels so he stopped. With a raised eyebrow, he asked, "What's wrong?"

I cocked my head and smiled. "You don't want to say goodbye to everyone?"

"Nah. We'll see 'em all later. Besides, I'm ready to get home and put Tillie to bed." He waggled his eyebrows at me. "If you know what I mean."

"I do but—"

"I love it when those words come out of your mouth."

"Funny."

"I know. I'm hilarious." Again he tugged me and again, I resisted. Aiden sighed.

"You seemed a little emotional when you saw Liam." I reached up and cupped his cheek. "I know it doesn't need to be said, but I'm so sorry you missed out on that with Tillie."

"Scarlett, don't. We're so far past that." The corners of his mouth quirked up. "But, if you're feeling the need to show me how sorry, you could come home with me and we could work hard on giving Tillie a sibling."

"Another one?"

A look of confusion crossed his features and I stood there, patiently, waiting for him to figure it out. I knew the second he did because he picked me up and spun me around.

"Seriously?" he asked when he set me back on my feet.

I nodded.

"How long have you known?"

"About a week. I didn't want to take any of the attention away from Griff and Brie." I lifted one shoulder, let it fall. "I was going to plan a big reveal for you, but seeing the way you looked at Griffin when he came out of the room holding Liam made me change my mind. I couldn't wait one more day."

"Oh, Sugar, I can't wait." There was wonder in his voice. "I love Tillie and wouldn't trade her for the world, you know that. But I'm finally going to get to experience it all."

"Yeah, you are. All the morning sickness, the swollen ankles, the endless trips to the bathroom, the cravings."

"The growing boobs, the round belly, the glow, the increased sex drive." When I smacked his arm, he just laughed. "Griffin told me all about it. Bragged about how much he got laid. Brie would castrate him if she knew that, so don't tell her, but man, now I get to return the favor."

"You are not discussing my boobs or our sex life with Griffin."

A blush crept into his cheeks, and I realized he already had. Many times. Men!

"Aw, Sugar, how'd I get so lucky?"

"You were you. No luck to it."

"I hope we have a boy. Tillie needs a brother." His eyes lit up as he went on and on about all the things he could teach a boy.

Seven months and twenty-four days later, Lila Rose Winters made her entrance into the world.

And Aiden was there for every second of the journey.

BONUS CHAPTER

Need more of Aiden and Scarlett? Sign up for my newsletter at andirhodes.com for an EXCLUSIVE bonus chapter, as well as updates on upcoming novels and giveaways

UP NEXT

If you liked the Broken Rebel Brotherhood series, be sure to stay tuned for my next series, Bastards and Badges. Book one of Bastards and Badges is Jackson's story. That's right... the hunky sheriff in the Broken Rebel Brotherhood series is getting his own book and let me tell you, it's hot!

ABOUT THE AUTHOR

Andi Rhodes is an author whose passion is creating romance from chaos in all her books! She writes MC (motorcycle club) romance with a generous helping of suspense and doesn't shy away from the more difficult topics. Her books can be triggering for some so consider yourself warned. Andi also ensures each book ends with the couple getting their HEA! Most importantly, Andi is living her real life HEA with her husband and their boxers.

For access to release info, updates, and exclusive content, be sure to sign up for Andi's newsletter at andirhodes.com.

ALSO BY ANDI RHODES

Broken Rebel Brotherhood

Broken Souls

Broken Innocence

Broken Boundaries

Broken Rebel Brotherhood: Complete Series Box set

Broken Rebel Brotherhood: Next Generation

Broken Hearts

Broken Wings

Broken Mind

Bastards and Badges

Stark Revenge

Slade's Fall

Jett's Guard

Soulless Kings MC

Fender

Joker

Piston

Gregor

Riker

Trainwreck

Squirrel

Gibson

Satan's Legacy MC

Snow's Angel

Toga's Demons

Magic's Torment

Printed in Great Britain
by Amazon